▓▓

SAM FLOOD WAS A "SURVIVOR" . . .

Which is why he managed to stay alive after the ship sank. There were others on his raft, but Flood took charge. He was that kind of man. And he lead them straight into a trap . . . a Japanese torpedo-boat base on the island of New Britain.

The Japanese turned their base into a prison camp. But Flood was determined to escape. Determined to return with help, free the prisoners, and blow up the base.

From the moment Flood did escape, the whole island was caught up in the aftermath.

Now with only a handful of men, a battered old plane, and a few grenades, Flood made his desperate move. To the others it was a suicide mission. Only Sam Flood had faith. But he needed a lot more than faith.

||||||||||||||||||||||||||||||||||||||||||||||||||||||||||||||||||||||||||||||||

Fawcett Gold Medal Books
by Ian MacAlister

DRISCOLL'S DIAMONDS

SKYLARK MISSION

STRIKE FORCE 7

SKYLARK MISSION

by
Ian
MacAlister

A FAWCETT GOLD MEDAL BOOK

Fawcett Publications, Inc., Greenwich, Conn.

SKYLARK MISSION

For my son, David

AREA INVOLVED IN SKYLARK MISSION

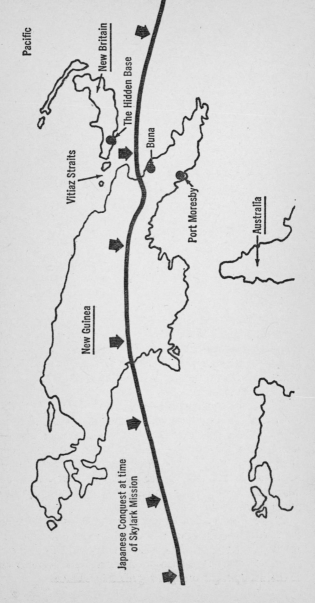

Pacific

New Britain

The Hidden Base

Vitiaz Straits

Buna

Port Moresby

New Guinea

Australia

Japanese Conquest at time
of Skylark Mission

In the first months after Pearl Harbor, the Japanese onslaught engulfed most of the southwest Pacific with a shocking swiftness. Invasion forces and convoys smashed south, scoring one lightning success after another, sinking every Allied warship that tried to stem the tide, knocking the small number of Allied planes out of the skies.

Before this onslaught thousands of civilians and military personnel fled south by sea, trying to reach Australia in any kind of vessel left afloat. But their only escape routes led through the narrow straits between the long chain of islands stretching from Sumatra in the west to the Solomons in the east. And the sea and sky around these straits were controlled by the enemy, who had already invaded every island in the chain.

There were a number of attempts to unbottle some of these straits—just long enough for trapped escape vessels to slip through with their human cargoes. This is the story of one of those attempts—improvised by a small group of ill-assorted people brought together by chance.

There was one man who had almost made good his escape, only to get stuck through carelessness directly in the path of the oncoming enemy in New Guinea. There was a woman trapped inside the enemy lines on New Britain, patiently waiting to be evacuated. There was a man running the gauntlet of the straits between these two islands, in a desperate bid for freedom. And there was another man who had already reached the safety of Australia, but lived only for a chance to return into the maelstrom. . . .

I

The
Trap

ONE

Sam Flood took his hands from the portside rail of the old freighter and brushed flakes of rust from his palms and fingers. His eyes continued to squint at the night-shrouded ocean, searching for the enemy he sensed was out there, but couldn't see.

The S.S. *Fleming* was working south through the Vitiaz Straits, between the southwest corner of New Britain and the northeast coast of New Guinea. It was headed for Australia, steaming at full speed in a desperate try at getting beyond the enemy warships, planes, and subs by dawn. The odds were against making it. That was why Flood wore his life jacket; as everyone on board was supposed to at all times, even when asleep.

The quiet on board the freighter this night had a dream-like quality to it. The only realities were the slush of the hull through the ocean, the throb and pound of the engines, the vibration of the deck under Flood's feet. And the faint prickling sensation along his spine, warning him . . .

He was a stocky, powerful man of thirty, with cynical eyes and a stubborn mouth in a blunt, hard-boned face. And there was a hint of something else about him: a quality of carefully controlled, locked-in violence. It was this that men spoke about when they conjectured on his past in waterfront bars around the Pacific. Some said that Flood wasn't his real name; that his papers bearing that name were either forged or stolen. According to the stories, he was wanted by the law under his real name. The stories varied, but centered around another man killed in a dockside brawl in the Caribbean. But it all remained conjecture. No one really *knew*.

All they ever knew about Sam Flood was that he'd been sailing merchant ships on Pacific runs for the past five years. That he was a good man to have with you on a job, and a bad man to have against you in a fight.

Flood turned from the port rail and made his way across the blacked-out deck. Moving between the two starboard lifeboats, he spread his feet a bit to absorb the sluggish dip and lift of the ship. There wasn't much wind, and not too much swell. But the *Fleming* was built tubby, round-bottomed for maximum cargo capacity, and it tended to roll in any kind of water.

Scanning the dark sea between the ship and the night horizon, Flood watched for any sign of an enemy vessel. His slitted eyes took in the heavy blackness of a high-rolling swell, a slithering snake of whiteness where the breeze sliced a wavetop into froth. But he failed to spot the low, dark shape some distance off the starboard quarter.

The *Fleming*'s cargo was ammunition and arms, originally destined for the defense of the Philippines. When that defense had caved in, the ship had been diverted south to Dutch New Guinea. Again it was too late. They had entered the harbor at Kotabaru only to find the Dutch evacuating. The Japanese had already managed a simultaneous invasion of New Guinea, New Britain, the Solomons, and New Ireland.

When the *Fleming* turned around and steamed out of Kotabaru, it was carrying seventy-nine passengers in addition to its cargo. Most of them were soldiers—Dutch,

American, Australian, British; members of the joint ABDA Force that had failed to stem the enemy tide, and was now being withdrawn for the defense of Australia. The rest were civilian refugees; British, Indonesian, Dutch, a few Americans. The women and children were quartered in the officers' cabins and saloon; the men had to bunk down as best they could on the open decks.

Since then the *Fleming* had become one of the many vessels caught in a closing trap, wandering back and forth behind the enemy lines, searching for a hole they could dodge through to the south. Each day the numbers of these vessels were cut down by Japanese dive bombers, warships, subs. Some of the ships that remained afloat had already begun heading into Japanese-held harbors to surrender, rather than be sunk with all aboard.

But the skipper of the *Fleming,* a crusty old Dutchman named DeGroot, wasn't the surrendering kind. He'd finally decided to risk this last-chance run through the Vitiaz Straits; at night, when the sky was relatively clear of enemy planes, and darkness lessened the probability of being spotted by enemy ships. A slim chance, but Flood backed DeGroot's decision. He knew he'd never emerge alive if he had to spend the rest of the war as a prisoner. He'd once done two weeks in a Hong Kong jail; one week more and he'd have gone berserk and killed a guard.

Flood knew what he couldn't take; but he also knew his own resourcefulness. If the *Fleming* got fished, it would still have brought him that much farther south. He'd make it the rest of the way on his own, if he had to. Overland through the jungles and mountains of New Guinea, or by way of a native boat stolen on New Britain. Either way, he intended to get through.

He suddenly became aware of someone quietly standing beside him. It was one of the passengers; one he'd noticed before. More than noticed; he'd had difficulty keeping his attention off her.

She was a young Filipino nurse, and he'd learned her name was Esther. It seemed a strangely plain name for so exotic a flower. He studied her as she gazed out at the ocean, feeling oddly awkward with her standing so close.

He wasn't ordinarily shy with women. There were whores and semihookers in a lot of port towns who could testify to that. But Esther was something outside his experience. He wasn't quite sure why. It had something to do with the vulnerability of her face when she met his eyes. The sweetness of her mouth, the openness of her huge dark eyes, and the sense of fragility to her slender, pliant figure. Just the look of her stirred him.

And her soft voice, when she spoke: "It's so beautiful, isn't it—the sea at night."

"Where's your life jacket?" Flood demanded harshly.

"It's so uncomfortable. I was trying to sleep. . . ."

"Get it and put it on. Now."

The harshness with which he said it didn't seem to disturb her. She smiled at him and nodded. "You're right, of course. I should. Thank you."

He watched her go into the saloon, and for a moment his face softened, becoming surprisingly young.

He glanced at his watch, squinting at the luminous dial. Time for one more turn around the deck before taking over up on the bridge. He strolled toward the stern, avoiding the huddled figures of men trying to catch some sleep on the decks and hatch covers. The ship was rolling a bit more now as it continued south through the night. Its taut metal skin trembled steadily, nervously. The vibration was a constantly felt countersensation to the pistoning of the engines in her bowels, the driving revolutions of the shaft, the forward-thrusting churn of the screw. . . .

Flood was knocked off his feet and sprawled to the deck before he registered the jarring explosion of the torpedo ramming into the forward hull. There was a deafening roar as the ammunition in number-two hold blew up, wrenching the entire ship and hurling Flood across the deck against a hatch. He grabbed at it with both hands and hung on, fighting to clear the dizziness from his brain.

The *Fleming* shuddered to a stop, its mangled bow lifting high out of the water, then crashing back down. The ocean began pouring into the gaping hole in the hull. The engines ceased in a volcano of gushing steam as the water rushed through a long rip in the bulkhead separating the engine room from number-two hold. The forward part of the ship began to sink swiftly, the stern with its stilled propeller lifting above the surface of the sea.

Flood dragged himself to his feet and made his way down the tilting deck of the dying ship, toward his emergency station, the forward lifeboat on the port side. Shadowy figures stumbled into him and clawed past him, yelling and screaming, blundering into each other. The entire boat deck was a shifting jumble of half-seen human confusion and terror. Flood shoved through them to his station. The forward lifeboat dangled, broken, from one davit. Instantly, he made for the other portside boat.

As he reached it, there was another explosion, directly below him in the bowels of the ship. He was thrown forward. His forehead struck glancingly across the solid bulk of a gravity davit as he tried to catch hold of the falls. He was only vaguely aware of going over the side and plunging downward. By the time he hit the water, he was unconscious.

When Flood came to, he was floating in the ocean, buoyed up by his life jacket. He had no way of knowing how long he'd been unconscious, but he came out of it all at once, knowing where he was and what had happened. His head hurt. His throat burned and his belly felt swollen from swallowed salt water. Nearby, men's voices cried out for help; and a woman was screaming, pleading for a lifeboat to come to her.

Flood couldn't see any boats or rafts. There were only the small dark shapes of other heads, bobbing in the water around him. It was impossible to make out in the night who they were, or even if they were men or women. Flood began turning in the water. He stopped when he saw the ship, and his danger.

The *Fleming*'s bow was buried under the water all the way to the partially submerged midships house. The dripping bulk of the hull aft of the house was out of the water. The old freighter was poised that way, its stern pointing at the sky, its final downward plunge checked only momentarily. And Flood was too damn close. He had to get farther away before it went under and sucked him down with it.

Quickly he reached down into the water and pulled off his shoes. He allowed himself the seconds needed to get it done without hesitating, in spite of the deadliness of delay. It was one of the things necessary to save his life, and he did it almost instinctively. Just as he kept on the life jacket, though it too would slow him down. Turning his back to the doomed ship, Flood began swimming steadily, fighting the drag of the life jacket, driving himself through the water with all his strength and egocentric lust to survive.

He'd gone about ten strokes when hands clutched at his life jacket and left arm, pulling him to a stop. Arms wrapped themselves around his neck. A voice gasped in his ear: "Help . . . no life jacket . . . help me. . . ."

It was Brockhaus, the third engineer. His added weight dragged them both down. Water lapped their faces. Flood wrenched himself in the fierce embrace of those thick arms, shoved both hands against Brockhaus's chest to break free. The single life jacket didn't have enough bouyancy for both of them. It wasn't his fault Brockhaus didn't have one, and Flood had no intention of dying for the other man's stupidity.

Brockhaus wouldn't let go. Flood closed his right fist and slammed it into the third engineer's meaty face, feeling teeth break under his knuckles. Brockhaus spat and snarled something. His arms loosened, but only to shift his hands to Flood's neck.

His strong fingers fastened on Flood's throat, thumbs digging in deep. Flood's air was shut off; the thudding pressure of his blood forced against the backs of his eyes.

Struggling together, they sank below the surface. Their legs kicked out wildly, driving them back up. The instant their heads broke surface, Flood pushed his left hand against the other man's chest as hard as he could, to get space between them. He drew back his right fist and clubbed Brockhaus across the temple, with all the power of his shoulders and arm behind it.

The third engineer's head sagged as though the tendons in his neck had been cut. Flood clubbed him again. Brock-

haus's hands slid from Flood's neck. For an instant his unconscious face was visible, floating away. Then it vanished
under a swell that lifted Flood.

Ignoring his tortured throat, Flood began swimming
again. But it was too late. Behind him, the *Fleming*'s midships house slid under the ocean. The stern heeled slightly
in the last moment, as though resisting the downward pull
of the rest of the ship. In the next moment the stern, too,
was gone.

Where the ship had been there was now only the night
through which it had steamed to its destruction—and a
spreading, gurgling, air-belching whirlpool.

The drowning pull of the ship settling into the depths of
the ocean reached for Flood and seized him. He struggled
to break free of its suction, and couldn't. He was caught
and spun around in a bubbling turmoil of water that inex-
orably drew him into the center of the whirlpool.

He gasped his lungs full of air and clamped his mouth
shut. Then he was entirely under water, being sucked
down by the pull of the drowned ship far beneath him.

He fought against its pull with stubborn, single-minded
determination. But the depths continued to clutch at him.
A crushing pressure began to squeeze his chest. His head
felt swollen. Needles of hot pain darted through his brain
and left clots of darkness behind them.

He ground his teeth together, refusing the suicidal de-
mands of his lungs. His mind became muddled and lost
control of his movements. But his arms and legs continued
to fight to get him to the surface, operated by a drive for
survival that persisted long after his brain had quit.

TWO

Flood suddenly became aware that his mouth was wide open. At first he thought it was sea water he was gasping into his lungs. Then his mind cleared, and he realized he had bobbed to the surface.

For a time he was content just to float in the embrace of his life jacket, indulging in the luxury of breathing air and resting his wearied body. The swelling current carried him away from the scene of the sinking. Somewhere in the distance, voices called out. Flood listened dully, but the voices were too far off for him to make out the words. Soon the voices grew fainter, and then he could no longer hear them at all.

He thought he slept. Then something bumped into him from behind, jolting him out of it. He twisted around. It was the body of a man, floating facedown in the water, most of his clothes burned off, the exposed flesh charred. Flood pushed at the body, watched a swell carry it away.

Off to his left a man with a British accent cried out: "Help! Over here! Wait!"

Flood looked toward the voice and saw, floating in their life jackets quite close to him, two fo the *Fleming*'s civilian passengers: a middle-aged couple named Burns. About fifty yards beyond them was an overcrowded life raft. Burns, a mining engineer, held onto one of his wife's hands as he waved his other hand at the raft and called out again: "Help! Back here!"

"We're full up!" a voice called back from the raft. "No more room!"

"Just take my wife!" Burns shouted. "Please—just her!"

"We can't! Almost swamped now! There's a boat behind you! Try for that!"

Flood turned to look behind him, squinting into the darkness. If there was a boat, he couldn't see it. When he turned back, the raft was being paddled away. Mr. and Mrs. Burns, still holding hands, had turned to look for the boat, and saw him.

"Is there a boat?" she asked Flood. Her voice was surprisingly calm, just the barest suggestion of a tremor in it.

"Apparently not," her husband said quietly. "I'm afraid he was lying, dear."

"Let's make sure." Flood wasted no more of his breath on words. Turning, he began stroking toward where the boat was supposed to be. He swam with a steady, powerful crawl, not looking back to see if they were following him.

The boat suddenly appeared, drifting aimlessly off to his right. Not one of the lifeboats; this was much smaller, a sailboat that had been lashed to the bridge. He hadn't been able to see it from farther away because it was barely afloat. The gunwales were only a few inches out of the water. Flood guessed it had been sucked down by the drowning ship, as he had been, which would account for its being empty.

Swimming toward it, Flood found another passenger, a plump Dutchman with round steel spectacles. Though only a few feet from the boat, he was making no effort to reach it; or to do anything. He was just floating there, buoyed by his life jacket, appearing to be in some kind of shock. Flood slapped his shoulder and pointed to the boat. The man just stared, not responding.

The boat lifted on the crest of a wave and vanished behind it. Holding down sudden panic, Flood swam past the Dutchman after it.

The wave settled, and the boat was still there, directly in front of him. Flood caught the grab lines and pulled himself to the side of the boat. It was almost completely filled with water. That it was floating at all meant the buoyancy tanks under the side benches were still intact. There was a man inside the boat, doubled over one of the waist thwarts with his head and legs under water.

Grasping the gunwale, Flood pulled himself along to the stern. There, he carefully hauled himself out of the ocean, into the boat. He wiped his hands across his dripping face and stood braced there for a few moments, experiencing a strange sense of quiet exultation.

Balancing warily, he stepped over the thwarts to the man huddled in the waist of the water-filled boat. The corpse wore the uniform of an American army lieutenant. There was no question that he was dead. Flood got his arms under the heavy body, raised it, and dumped it over the gunwale into the ocean. The level of water inside the boat went down just a bit; to below Flood's knees.

Going back to the stern, he knelt in the water and examined by touch the tangle of gear stowed on the bottom boards, secured by lanyards. He found what he wanted, the bucket. Unshackling it, he emptied it over the side. Then he spread his feet wide, crouched holding the bucket with both hands, and began bailing.

He worked at it with single-minded dedication, establishing an efficient rhythm that he continued without pausing for rest. The level of water inside the boat went down, but very slowly.

A wide-shouldered Australian army private suddenly appeared beside the boat.

" 'Lo, chum. Look like you're enjoying yourself. Can I come in and play, too?"

"This is the only bucket," Flood told him.

"I still got my boots on. And the biggest feet in Melbourne."

Flood stopped his bailing and straightened a bit, dangling the bucket in one hand. He reached down with his other and helped haul the Australian aboard. "Easy now . . . just roll over into the boat. . . . That's the way." Flood sat him down in the middle of the boat, so he wouldn't overbalance it while bailing. He was a huge man, and the boot he took off was almost as big as he'd boasted.

"Name's Soames," he said as he began to bail water out of the boat with the boot.

Flood supplied his own name and resumed bailing with the bucket.

He paused again as Mr. and Mrs. Burns came into view, swimming slowly side by side to the boat.

"Don't hang onto the gunwale," he snapped at them. "Just grab the line there and hold on for a while."

As they obeyed, an ocean swell brought the Dutchman drifting back into sight.

"Over here!" Soames called to him.

He continued to float where he was, as though he hadn't heard.

"Something's the matter with him," Mrs. Burns said.

Her husband nodded. "Shock, probably." He let go and swam to the Dutchman. The Dutchman neither resisted nor helped as he was pulled and pushed to the boat. When Burns closed the man's hands around the grab lines, he didn't let go; but his dazed eyes continued to stare through the steel-rimmed glasses at something that wasn't there.

The boat rose slowly as Flood and Private Soames continued their steady bailing. Flood's clothes, which had begun to dry in the hot night air, became sodden again with his sweat. His stomach was churning from all the salt water he'd swallowed. Finally he had to pause in his bailing to lean over the side and throw up. That relieved the nausea, but it also weakened him a bit. He spat a couple times to clear his mouth of salt and bile, and resumed bailing.

When the boat was half empty, they pulled Mrs. Burns aboard. The first thing she did was to vomit over the gunwale. As she finished, and slumped wearily on the forepeak, three soldiers swam up alongside. One of them Flood knew from aboard ship: a U.S. Marine sergeant named Leary, a solid hulk of a man. The other two were privates: one British, the other Dutch.

The boat was buoyant enough now for Sergeant Leary and the Dutch soldier to climb in and take over the bailing. That freed Flood to begin rigging the boat for sailing, with Private Soames's help. Setting up the mast was easy enough, but the rigging and sails had become badly tangled, and the Australian was completely baffled about what went where. Flood was relieved when the next survivor to appear turned out to be one of the *Fleming*'s deck hands, a Malay seaman named Tengal.

After Tengal slid aboard and took over from Soames, it went faster. Between them, Flood and Tengal got the rigging secured and the sails in position for hoisting by the time the bailing was finished. The bottom boards were now practically clear of water, and no leaks showed anywhere. Burns, the Dutchman, and the British private were helped aboard. Burns slumped beside his wife, exhausted. The Dutchman sat exactly where he was placed, not moving, still in a world of his own.

Flood methodically took stock and found there were only two oars, the others having been torn away when the boat was dragged under. He gave the oars to the strongest-looking men, Soames and the British soldier. Some of the provisions that had been secured in the boat were also gone, along with the compass. All that was left was one tin of hard biscuits, and a single tank of drinking water. Flood assigned Sergeant Leary the job of doling out the first ration of water.

"Count on us picking up more survivors," he warned him. "And allow for a three-day voyage."

The sergeant sized Flood up as he nodded. "Sure. But don't tell me to do it like you're issuing orders. So far, I'm the senior military man on this boat."

"Can you sail it?" Flood asked him quietly. "Can you navigate so we reach where we want to go? Without a compass?"

"What's that got to do with it?"

"I can," Flood told him flatly. "So I'm in command of this boat. Get used to the idea."

Leary's retort was cut off by Mrs. Burns: "Please, Sergeant, may I have a drink soon? My throat is on fire from all the salt I've swallowed."

The sergeant shut up and began the delicate task of doling out rations of water. Flood had a feeling, as he took his place in the stern, that Mrs. Burns had been not so desperate for a drink as anxious to prevent a fight.

Gripping the tiller, Flood studied the sky. Still a long way to go before dawn. He searched the dark sea around them. No one else was in sight.

Looking at his watch, he was relieved to see it was still working. Miraculously, it was as waterproof as advertised. He checked the time, then looked up again, studying the stars, establishing a rough estimate of their position.

"Start rowing," he told the two oarsmen. "The rest of you take turns calling out. We got a little time to pick up more survivors. If there are any."

As they did so, he began steering the boat in a widening circle.

The first response was a woman calling from the darkness off to their left: "Here! We're over here!"

Flood recognized her voice with a jolt of pleasure. She'd managed to get into her life jacket in time. . . .

"Keep yelling!" he called back.

Soames and the British soldier pulled hard at the oars as Flood steered toward her voice. They found Esther in the water with three others: a beautiful Dutch woman named Mrs. Rüyter, and her two children, a boy of eight and a daughter three years older. They were floating in a tight circle, their hands joined.

The children were pulled into the boat; then the two women. Esther stared at Flood, then forced a weak smile. "You keep saving me. . . ."

Flood's smile was grim. "Still think the sea's beautiful at night?"

Her laugh was a dry croak. "Not this close."

Leary said: "If any've you're thirsty, I'm the bartender."

Esther continued to look at Flood for a moment, before following Mrs. Ruyter and the children to get her ration. After she'd had it, she made her way back through the boat, and settled down in the stern near Flood.

In the next two hours, they picked up nine more survivors, all men: a Javanese merchant, an American oil driller, a Eurasian planter, five more troopers, and a handsome, fair-haired boy of about fifteen.

Through it all, the plump Dutchman with the steel-rimmed glasses continued to sit trancelike, cut off from the others in the boat; until the fair-haired boy climbed in, saw him, and cried out: "Papa!"

The Dutchman stared at him unbelievingly. Then he began to sob, the tears running down his cheeks as he clutched the boy to him. He continued to cry unashamedly, as his son patted him on the back as though comforting a baby.

There were now twenty-two people in the boat. And it was time for a hard decision. Flood looked at the sky.

"That's all," he announced in a dead-flat voice. He looked to Tengal crouched by the mast. "Let's get these sails up."

Sergeant Leary turned on him. "Hold it! We've got room for more."

Flood nodded. "We've got the room, but not the time."

"There's bound to be more survivors swimming around here," Leary said coldly. "If we abandon the search now, they're dead. That could include some women and kids."

Flood met Leary's accusing stare stonily. "Can't be helped. It'll be dawn in four hours. That's barely time enough for us to get tucked away out of sight somewhere along the south coast of New Britain."

"Are you nuts?" the sergeant exploded. "New Britain's in Jap hands."

"There's no way they can patrol the swamps along that coast. Perfect place to hide."

"It's New *Guinea* we ought to head for. Where it's still in Aussie hands. The east end, what do they call it? . . ."

"Papua," Soames volunteered.

"We can't get anywhere near there in four hours," Flood explained with fraying patience. "You want to spend the whole day out in the open on the water? So one of their planes can spot us, and chop us to pieces? Not me. Anybody wants to go that route, start swimming."

Flood punctuated it by getting up and helping Tengal with the hoisting of the mainsail.

Burns spoke up uncertainly: "You really believe our chances are better, sailing right into enemy territory?"

"Once we're inside those swamps, they can't find us." Flood's voice got a hard finality to it. "We'll hole up there through the day. And have all of tomorrow night to reach Papua. Or get damn close."

Sergeant Leary was watching him. When he spoke again, it was with surprising restraint. "All right, you're the skipper of this boat. You want the responsibility, it's yours. You'd better be right."

Flood said nothing. With the mainsail up, he returned to the tiller. Tengal let out the jib as the oars were shipped. Wind filled the sails, tugging the boat forward. Flood steered southeast out of the Vitiaz Straits.

Sergeant Leary's words had gotten to him. He examined the unaccustomed feeling uneasily as he looked at the others in the boat. Twenty-one people; his responsibility. He'd had to choose between two dangers. He had chosen the lesser one, considering the odds. But he knew too well that the odds weren't always right.

He kept a sharp lookout through the rest of the night. But he didn't spot any of the other lifeboats or rafts. Most of the others in the boat napped from time to time. Flood did not. He stayed at the tiller, shaking his head at Tengal's offer to spell him. Checking his watch and the position of the stars, he sailed a more easterly course after a time, toward where he estimated the southwestern coast of New Britain should be.

An hour later he smelled it: the odor of jungle and swamp coming faintly across the water to him. He still couldn't see the land through the night, and he didn't want to. Veering slightly, he held to a course that kept him within smell of the land, and just out of sight of it. The important thing was to be close enough to nip in quickly and hide at dawn, but not close enough to risk ramming a coastal reef in the dark.

By now the tropical heat had dried him completely. His clothes were stiff with salt, irritating his salt-burned skin. His eyes were burning too, and spitting didn't clear all the salt taste from his mouth. From time to time he tried to wet his dry, cracked lips with his tongue, but that didn't help much either.

He forced his mind away from the physical discomforts and looked down at Esther. She was curled up asleep beside him, her head resting on his thigh. Though she slept a long time, her head remained curiously light.

By the time the first pinkish predawn glow began to finger the sky, Flood's body was heavy with weariness, his shoulders aching and his legs stiff. The others lay still sleeping in cramped positions, salt crusted on their faces. The growing light showed no other vessel anywhere around them. But it did reveal, slowly, their destination: the coast of New Britain, with morning mist rising from the mangrove swamps along the shore and the jungle-clad mountains of the interior.

Tengal woke as soon as Flood veered toward the land, and quickly got ready to reef the sails. Sergeant Leary was the next to awake, straightening beside the water tank and squinting at the land.

He looked back at Flood. "That it?"

Flood nodded.

"Better get in fast. You're the one didn't want us out in the open in daylight."

Others began to wake up, jarred by Leary's voice.

Esther sat up beside Flood's knee and looked around her in surprise. "It's day. . . ."

"Not yet." Flood pointed ahead. "We'll be safe inside by the time the sun's up."

He was almost right.

The rim of the sun was just edging above the horizon as the boat reached a stretch of dense, tall mangroves growing out of the water along the shore. Flood angled along the edge of the swamp. He ordered Soames and the British private to get ready with the oars as he searched for a way in where the keel wouldn't snag on the exposed, outreaching mangrove roots.

Sergeant Leary scowled into the murky depths of the swamp, his nostrils pinching as the rank, primeval smell of rot reached out to them. "Stinks . . . but it *is* a hell of a place to stay hid," he admitted grudgingly.

Then Flood saw it: a wide opening leading in through the swamp, where the muddy brown water of a jungle river poured out into the green of the shallow sea. Tengal brought down the sail, and the boat was propelled more slowly by the oars as Flood steered into the opening between the mangroves.

The deeper in they went, the better it looked as a hiding place. The high thick foliage of the trees on either side almost met above them. It was like going through a dim, watery tunnel. Five minutes rowing, and the swamp gave way to solid ground on either side. They were into jungle now, with almost solid green walls of vegetation on both banks.

Flood steered the boat around a tight bend in the narrow river, hunting for a place to land. Then he froze, his guts knotting.

He had made a mistake. The odds had been wrong.

There was a small clearing on the right bank ahead. In it, a Japanese marine camp was in the process of being built. At the water's edge an old dock had already been reconstructed. Tied to it, behind a small coastal tanker, were two Japanese copies of an early-model British motor torpedo boat. Long, powerful craft, sleek-lined for maximum speed. Each with a 20-mm automatic cannon bolted to the top of the low cabin, two machine guns aft, and a torpedo tube on either side.

It hadn't been a sub that had sunk the *Fleming,* after all.

Sergeant Leary registered the expression on Flood's face and twisted to look in the same direction. He turned back to face Flood with a flat stare. Flood ignored it. He didn't need the accusation in Leary's eyes to tell him what his mistake had done to them all.

There was a deep-throated engine-roar from the swamp behind them. Flood turned to look, his face wooden. A third Japanese MTB was coming in from the ocean. Its sharp bow lifted slightly out of the muddy water, and its wake foamed out to either side in long graceful curves as it closed in on the boatload of survivors.

THREE

Sweat gleamed on Flood's face and plastered his clothes to his body as he squatted in the dirt under the scorching tropical sun, eating the meal provided by the commander of the marine base: an unappetizing but nourishing mixture of rice and fish that served as the Japanese trooper's basic diet in the field. He ate quickly, with his fingers, swatting away the flies that would otherwise have been carried into his mouth with the food.

He was in the open with the other sixteen men, guarded by three suspicious Japanese troopers holding automatic rifles at the ready. Esther, Mrs. Burns, Mrs. Ruyter, and the two Ruyter children were more comfortable. They were eating in the veranda shade of a bungalow that served as the base commander's headquarters, watched by a fourth armed guard. The commander was inside the bungalow, radioing his superiors in Rabaul to find out what he was supposed to do about his unexpected, and unwelcome, prisoners.

Flood had been in the South Pacific long enough to ignore the sweltering heat and the horde of flying insects buzzing around him, because nothing else could be done about either. Some of the other men did not have his tolerance. Mr. Burns, especially, being the oldest among them, seemed to wilt and shrivel before their eyes under the dense weight of the hot sunlight. He barely managed to finish half his food. The rest he passed on to the Dutchman's fifteen-year-old son, who wolfed it down gratefully.

Flood finished his own meal, and used handfuls of dirt to clean the foodstains and sweat from his fingers. Then he settled on the ground with his back against a tree stump, looking sleepy, his eyes narrowed against the sun's glare as he took in the layout of the marine camp. It was there as a supply base for the motor torpedo boats moored at the repaired dock. There were four of them now, another having come in a short time ago.

Evidently the torpedo boats prowled the Vitiaz Straits all night, sinking any Allied ships trying to slip through in the darkness. By day they holed up here and left the patrolling of the straits to land-based planes and destroyers.

Next to the dock, moored against the river bank, was a small coastal tanker, from which the MTB's were refueled. Behind it was the hulk of a torpedoed freighter, which had been towed in and grounded against the bank, the big hole in its destroyed engine room submerged under the muddy river water. On this hulk were the supplies, ammunition, and torpedoes for the four boats. It was also serving as quarters for the men of the base, until the camp could be completed in the clearing.

Only the dock and the bungalow with its wide veranda had been there before. The rest was still being hastily improvised. So far the base garrison had constructed a watch tower, a maintenance shed for repairing and servicing the torpedo boats, and a shelter that consisted of a raised platform-floor, six tall poles, and a roof of thatched palm leaves. The troopers not on guard duty with the prisoners were at work building two similar shelters.

Flood noticed Tengal eyeing the jungle that enclosed the clearing. It was easy enough to guess his thoughts: If Tengal could escape into that jungle, he'd manage to survive. Flood didn't think much of the chances of any of the others.

He glanced at the brownish river. The water moved swiftly past on its way to the ocean, indicating it came from high up in the mountains of the interior. The opposite bank was another solid wall of tangled vines, ferns, and towering jungle trees enmeshed with parasitic growths.

Flood abruptly switched his attention back to the bungalow. The base commander had come out onto the veranda, beside the three women and two children. He stood with his hands gripped together behind him, taking in the male prisoners with heavily controlled irritation. He was tall for a Japanese, built broad and strong. His voice was slow and hard as he addressed them.

The Dutchman with the steel-rimmed spectacles rose to his feet quickly. He was the only one among them fluent enough in Japanese to translate: "He wants us all to stand, to show respect for his rank."

The Dutchman was no longer the abject, helpless man they had fished out of the water. He was solid and businesslike, making the translation into carefully precise English.

One by one, the men stood up, the Dutchman's son helping Burns to his feet.

Soames, standing beside Flood, eyed the Japanese commander with malice and drawled: "I'd like to show him some respect—with a nice sharp bayonet up his arse."

"Shut up," Leary growled softly. "He just might know some English."

When they were all standing, the commander began addressing them again. The harsh drag of his voice revealed how difficult it was for him to deal patiently with their unwanted intrusion into his already heavy responsibilities.

The Dutchman translated as he spoke, quickly and quietly. The gist of it was that the commander had spoken by radio with his superiors in Rabaul, at the other end of New Britain; and they had passed the buck back to him. They were busy mopping up the north coast, and wouldn't be able to spare enough soldiers to come and take away the prisoners for a long time. Until then, the commander of this base would have to deal with them as best he could.

The problem was, the commander explained, that he had no proper facilities for keeping prisoners and not enough men to guard them adequately around the clock. He barely had enough men to run the base, build the camp, and patrol the nearby inland areas. But he was a humane man, he told them; as far as the conditions of war allowed any military officer to be humane. He didn't have the heart to deal with them in what for him would be the simplest way: Killing unarmed prisoners in cold blood was something he wouldn't relish.

So he had considered the problem and come up with a temporary solution that would serve—as long as they all remembered to remain at all times properly humble, obedient, and respectful. The three women and two children would be housed in the first shelter which had already been built. The male prisoners would be put to work helping to build the base camp, which would at least be some return for the trouble and food they would be costing him. It would also free some of his men to guard them, and others to join his inland patrols.

Each day they would work. All day. At night they would be taken aboard the grounded hulk, and put down inside part of the forward hold which was presently empty. This was the one place where they could be kept securely without having to be carefully guarded all night. The ladders from the hold to the deck would be cut away. They would enter and leave the hold by way of a cargo net which would be lowered into the hold for them. Once down inside it, the deck hatch covers would be secured over them for the night, and there would be no way they could escape.

The commander's last words before putting them to work were a warning: "Do not mistake my humanity for weakness. Any attempt to abuse my hospitality will be answered with swift, merciless reprisal!"

With that, the commander barked a short order to a lieutenant who stood at attention in the sunlight below him. Then he went back inside the bungalow. The lieutenant snapped orders to the three armed guards. The guards began herding the male prisoners toward some picks and shovels waiting near one edge of the clearing. Their first job was to dig latrines for the camp.

They were kept at work for the rest of that day, digging in the smothering heat, with no break for lunch. Burns managed to last until almost noon. Then the shovel slipped from his hands and he collapsed to his knees, his head sagging. One of the guards advanced on him threateningly. Soames and the Dutchman quickly dragged Burns back up to his feet. From then on they kept him between them, helping to hold him up so he could at least go through the motions of continuing to dig along with them. An hour later the Javanese merchant suddenly began vomiting. The guard nearest to him watched impassively until the spasms subsided, then prodded the merchant back to work with a bayonet point.

As they worked, Sergeant Leary exchanged whispers with the other troopers, sizing up the situation and their chances. The torpedo boats at the dock were a mocking temptation. One of them could carry all the prisoners all the way to Australia. But even if they could surprise and overwhelm the three guards watching them, their chances of getting on one of those boats were so slim as to be suicidal. There were two sentries posted on top of the watch tower with a heavy machine gun, more enemy troopers between them and the river, and a gun crew constantly manning a machine gun on one of the torpedo boats. They'd be slashed to ribbons before they could reach the dock.

Sam Flood didn't join in the whispered discussions. He continued to work silently. He listened, studied the routine of the base camp, counted the troopers manning it, and kept his thoughts to himself.

It wasn't until dusk that a halt was called to the day's work and they were given another meal. Once more they were fed apart from the women and children, who had been settled down on the bare platform boards of the first shelter. And again the meal was rice mixed with fish, plus hot tea. Flood made a quick job of the rice and tea. But though he was ravenous, he left the fish alone. Dysentery was the one thing he didn't want at this point. He was going to need his strength.

Sipping the last of his tea, Flood sat back on his heels and studied the condition of the other men. They were all drained from the heat and exhaustion. But beyond that, four of them were already showing symptoms of illness. One of the British troopers had a glazed, shaky look. So did the Javanese merchant and the American oil driller. Burns was the worst. He stretched out on the ground unable to eat anything, and his food was finally shared out among the others. Soames and the Dutchman, who had taken on the job of nursing him, managed to get Burns to drink his tea. And when it was time for them to be locked up for the night, they had to half carry him up the gangplank onto the deck of the grounded hulk.

Following the commander's orders, the ladders into the empty section of the forward hold had been cut away. As the armed guards herded them to the open hatch, a cargo net was lowered for them to climb down by. Flood was the first to reach the bottom; followed closely by Sergeant Leary. They quickly used the last of the murky light from above to investigate their prison. The hold was small and totally bare; just solid iron flooring, solid iron sides.

There was only one possibility: a single closed bulkhead hatch to an adjacent hold. Together, Flood and Leary put their weight against it. It didn't budge. Flood shook his head and stepped back.

"Secured from the other side. No way to open it from in here."

Leary rang his knuckles against its heavy iron surface, disgustedly. "And we sure as hell can't break it down."

In the few seconds left to them they searched the rest of the hold to make double sure. There was no other possible exit.

By then the last of the male prisoners had reached the bottom of the hold. The cargo net was drawn up hastily, and the hatch cover was lowered into place. The sudden darkness inside the hold was total. Flood touched his right eyebrow with his fingertips, and couldn't see his hand move. The prisoners began settling down awkwardly, by feel, as they listened to the sounds of the deck hatch being secured above them. They were sealed in for the night.

Sergeant Leary lowered himself beside Flood, touching him. "Could you handle one of them torpedo boats out there?" he asked quietly.

"Forget it. We don't have a prayer of grabbing one."

"If we did . . . could you run it?"

Flood nodded, then remembered Leary couldn't see him. "I can handle any kind of boat there is. Why? You figured out a way to get us all on board one?"

Leary was silent for a long moment. Then, grudgingly: "No. Not yet I haven't, anyway."

Soames's voice sounded, on Flood's left: "We've got a better chance of escape inland. It's a big island. They don't have enough men to track us all down."

"We're not making any mass break in that direction," Leary told him flatly. "They'd cut down too many of us before we could get far enough away through the jungle. And some of the ones they hit could be the women and kids."

Soames sighed unhappily. "It's a crook deal for sure."

"Suppose one man could escape?" Flood said slowly, half to himself. "If he could steal a boat from some fishing village and manage to reach Port Moresby—I got a hunch they'd be damn interested in this base."

"Why?" the oil driller demanded weakly. "There's too few of us for them to bother about. They've got *thousands* like us, stuck farther north, to worry about."

"I know," Flood said. "That's why they'll be interested. If they can knock out this base, and those torpedo boats, it could open up the Vitiaz Straits for at least one night. A lot of those people to the north'd be able to get through, along with us."

"Perhaps you did not believe the warning the commander of this base gave us?" That was the Dutchman's voice. And the voice was angry. *"You* are responsible for us being prisoners here in the first place. And now you want to incite that Japanese officer to have some of us executed. That is what he will certainly do, if anyone escapes."

Flood said nothing to that. Basically, the man was right.

But surprisingly, Leary sided with Flood: "That's better than just staying stuck here and dying slow. Look at Burns, after just one day. Half of us'll be dead before they ever get around to taking us to any real prisoner camp. And I don't figure on any Jap prisoner camp being a picnic, either."

"My sentiments, exactly," one of the troopers growled, and there were other murmurs of agreement. "Thing is, who's gonna make the try? And *how?*"

"Can't be done under cover of darkness," Soames put in thoughtfully. "No way to squeeze out've this hole all night. And by day they're watching us pretty damn close in that clearing. Look trigger happy to me, those guards."

"We'll restudy the possibilities tomorrow," Leary decided. "While we're working out there. We'll try to work it out from a different angle this time—with a one-man escape in mind, instead of a mass break. Right?"

He nudged Flood for confirmation. Flood grunted in response; a sound that committed him to nothing.

Flood was already stretched out on the hard metal of the hold's bottom, uninterested in further talk. Hands laced under his head, he lay there with his eyes open in the dark for some time, thinking. Then he closed his eyes and went to sleep.

A grating metallic sound jarred into Flood's sleeping brain and woke him. His eyes snapped open and saw nothing. The hold was still a solid mass of impenetrable darkness. He listened until he identified the sounds above: The bolts securing the hatch cover were being loosened.

Quickly, he squeezed his eyes shut. There were groans of pain from some of the other men who hadn't, as the hatch cover was pulled away and glaring sunlight stabbed down at them. Even with his eyes tightly shut, Flood could see the difference. He sat up, bent his head forward, shaded his eyes with both hands, and carefully slitted them open. Even that way, the sudden glare hurt. He waited until his eyes adjusted and the hurt ebbed. Then he lowered his hands and raised his head.

The cargo net had already been lowered into the hold and a guard was shouting down at them from the deck above. The prisoners began climbing the net, Leary and the Dutchman leading the way. Burns was improved enough from his night of rest to make it to the top with a little help from Soames. Flood rose to his feet, slowly. He reached both arms high above his head, and stretched until his spine cracked, loosening the cramp of a night on the metal flooring. Then he did several deep knee bends, getting the blood flowing in his legs. The last of the other men were climbing the net. Flood moved to it, taking his time.

There were four armed guards supervising the transfer of the male prisoners from the hulk to the clearing. Two were at the bottom of the gangplank, watching the men as they came down to solid ground. A third was at the top of the gangplank, hurrying them off the hulk. The fourth was beside the top of the opened hold. Flood climbed off the top of the cargo net beside him, onto the deck. He linked both hands and stretched again. The guard turned his head and peered down into the hold, to make sure there were no more prisoners left below.

Flood's foot shot out sideways and kicked the guard's ankles out from under him. At the same time he twisted and clubbed the back of the guard's head with his interlocked fists. The guard toppled into the hold with a scream. Flood was already on the move before the scream was cut short with the crunching sound of the guard hitting bottom.

He sprinted around the hatch covers and across the deck, in the opposite direction from the gangplank. There were shouts behind him, then the harsh clatter of an automatic rifle as the other deck guard sent a snap burst after his fleeing figure. Bullets clanged on the deck beside Flood's hard-pumping legs. He crouched and kept running. Before the guard could recover from his surprise and send a more carefully aimed blast at him, Flood was around the corner of the deck house, momentarily protected by it.

He kept going until he reached the rail and dove over

without stopping. Just before hitting the brown surface of the river he sucked his lungs full of air. Then he was under the water, going deep. He continued downward until his hands touched the ooze of the bottom. Then he began swimming, staying deep as he held his breath, angling toward where he judged the opposite bank to be. He could hear and feel bullets plunging into the river above him. But he didn't bother to dodge, knowing they couldn't see him through the muddy brown water. He kept swimming under water until his lungs couldn't take it anymore. Then he let himself rise.

The instant his head cleared the water his ears were stuffed with the staccato roaring of a machine gun and several automatic rifles. Bullets splattered the surface of the river, homing in on his exposed head. Flood located the opposite bank, filled his lungs with fresh air, and swam down toward the bottom again.

This time he kept going under water until his head struck an outreaching tree root. Grasping it, he pulled himself against the soft mud of the river bank. Getting his legs doubled under him, he straightened abruptly, standing up waist-deep in the water. There was a lush mass of ferns inches from his dripping face. Lowering his head, he drove himself up out of the mud of the river bank and bulled his way in through them. Bullets ripped the towering ferns on either side of him and buzzed past his ears. He shoved deeper through the tropical underbrush, away from the river, leaving a clear trail behind him where he had broken through.

Panting with exertion, he shoved on through the thickening brush, until a tangle of vines stopped him. He dropped flat to the ground and slithered under the barrier of vines on his chest and stomach. When he was past it, he got to his hands and knees, and crawled. He was into the gloom of the rain forest now, the interlacing branches of tall trees high above him blocking out the sunlight. It was like being in the maze of a cave. A cave from whose floor grew mammoth mushroomlike growths and thick tree trunks entangled in vines and festooned with a dazzling myriad of multicolored flowers. Flood paused and rose in a crouch, still panting; with fear more than exertion now. He looked around him.

He changed direction, moving very carefully now, leaving no trail to indicate where he had gone. Following a semicircular route, he turned back toward the river.

When he could hear the sound of the water, he went to his hands and knees and crawled under the brush, keeping very low so as not to break any of the vegetation above him. Reaching the riverside ferns, he stretched out flat and snaked the rest of the way under them. He stopped when he reached the edge, hidden by the ferns but able to peer through them across the river.

Two rubber boats were being paddled across from the base, about fifty yards apart, loaded with armed enemy troopers. They reached the bank on either side of the place where Flood had disappeared into the jungle. Leaving only one man with each boat, the rest of the troopers scurried off onto the bank and plunged in along his trail, hunting him.

Flood stayed where he was, waiting. He didn't think they'd find the place where he had doubled back. They'd follow the clear trail he'd left until it petered out, search around there awhile, and then concentrate their search deeper inland, figuring he would have kept on going. Flood lay motionless, sweat dripping steadily from his face and body into the damp earth, his heart thudding against the ground, his teeth clamped shut to still the sound of his breathing.

From his vantage point he could see past the bow of the grounded hulk on the other side of the river, to the clearing of the enemy camp. All the prisoners were lined up in the middle of the clearing, including the women and children. Ten Japanese troopers stood facing them with leveled rifles. The commander was pacing back and forth, addressing them. It was too far away for Flood to hear what he was saying, but finally he stopped pacing and made an abrupt motion. The Dutchman stepped from the line and walked stiffly to the river edge, a soldier marching behind him with a rifle to his back.

The Dutchman stopped, sunlight glinting off his spectacles as he stared across the river in Flood's general direction. He cupped his hands around his mouth and began shouting: "Mr. Flood! Can you hear me? If you can hear me, please come back! If you do not, two of us will be shot! You must surrender yourself in two minutes! Please!"

The Dutchman lowered his hands but continued to stare hopefully across the river, waiting.

Flood stayed where he was.

Two minutes went by, with incredible swiftness. The base commander raised a hand and spoke again. The Dutchman's shoulders slumped dejectedly. He was marched back to the line of prisoners. The commander snapped his orders, pointing. Two of the male prisoners were pulled from the line. Burns and the Javanese merchant. The commander had obviously been advised that they had proved themselves the least fit for work the previous day.

Flood watched the two of them being placed apart from the others, but where the others would be able to see what happened to them. Mrs. Burns started to run forward toward her husband. A guard caught her by the arm and dragged her back roughly. Esther put her arms around Mrs. Burns and held her tight as two troopers with submachine guns took their positions in front of the two hostages. Mrs. Ruyter was holding her children close, hiding their eyes with her hands. Esther tried to turn Mrs. Burns's head away, but the woman wrenched her face free and turned it toward her husband and the Javanese merchant.

The Japanese lieutenant stepped forward, very erect, and snapped the order. The executioners raised their submachine guns. The heavy bursts from the guns carried clearly across the river. So did Mrs. Burns's cry of grief and horror.

Flood stayed where he was.

The commander snapped orders and stalked back to his bungalow headquarters. The remaining male prisoners were herded off to begin their day's work, more heavily guarded now. The women and children were taken back to their shelter. The two bodies were left sprawled in the middle of the clearing.

Two hours later one boatload of enemy troopers returned from their fruitless hunt for Flood. He watched them get wearily back into the rubber boat. As they rowed across the river to their base, he made his decision. The other boatload of troops were still hunting for him. But by now they'd be searching miles away, not in this direction. It was time to move out.

He slithered back through the dense ferns. When he was clear of the thickest underbrush he rose to his feet, turned his back on the river, and started walking.

What he wanted was a coastal village; the kind that would be likely to have a boat he could steal during the night. But first he angled farther inland through the rain forest, aiming toward the hills. To cut straight to the coast from here meant going into that mangrove swamp. And a man floundering around in one of those swamps wasn't likely to ever get out. What he needed now was to get to high ground, from which he could see the coast and chart a course to it that would avoid the swampy areas.

It became difficult for him to keep his sense of direction accurately. The ground was mostly level; the entangled tree foliage high above cut him off from the position of the sun; and underbrush higher than his head in places made it impossible to see more than a few yards in any direction at any time. He concentrated on keeping to a straight line. But barriers of dense brush and tangled vines made this impossible. Each time he had to detour around these barriers he could only make a rough guess at his original line of direction.

The ground finally began to rise, and he moved on more swiftly despite his weariness, thinking he was at last reaching the foothills. But an hour later the ground began to dip, and by then night was closing in.

Darkness comes quickly at dusk inside a rain forest. In the last faint light, Flood sank down exhausted against the trunk of a tree. Praying there were no poisonous snakes or spiders around, he let his eyes close and fell into a dead sleep.

He awoke in total darkness, with night creatures of the jungle making sounds all around him. It was pain that had wakened him. The bare flesh of his face, arms, and feet was burning from the stings of mosquitoes swarming over him. He lurched to his feet cursing viciously, slapping wildly at the insects, crushing them under his hands. More came to take their place.

Lurching away from this place of torment, he kept slapping at himself until the plague of mosquitoes abated. He stumbled into a tangle of brush and vines, disentangled himself, and kept walking, dazed.

His legs became numb after a time. So numb that he was ankle deep in marsh water before he realized he was no longer on firm ground. He stopped dead, a jolt of panic getting him. Very carefully, he turned around and tried to go back in the exact same direction he'd come from. The blackness of the night defeated him. It was impossible to walk in a straight line. The swamp water rose to his thighs. He changed direction again, pushing himself desperately through the water, getting entangled again and again in low-hanging vines.

Thirst was clawing at his throat now. He had to fight against drinking the swamp water he was trying to escape. Roots caught his feet and tripped him. He fell in the water, going under. He came up sputtering, wiping the swamp slime from his face. Leeches were on him now, sucking tightly to his arms and legs. And the mosquitoes were back. His mind began to retreat from him. But his legs kept driving him on; blindly, slowly, each step a separate effort.

When he came out of the swamp, he didn't know it. His whole body was burning and shaking with fever. He kept moving, like a broken robot that hadn't quite run down and didn't know how to turn itself off. He was only vaguely aware of walking straight into a tree and falling down at last. It didn't hurt.

He lay where he had fallen, twitching feverishly, open eyes staring up at the last faint stars of the night sky without seeing them.

When the sun came up, he felt a warmth without understanding what was causing it. Nor did he understand, some time later, the boots that came to a halt beside him; and the rifle muzzle that prodded his chest.

FOUR

Nora Ferguson dug her husband's grave behind heavy brush near the spot where she'd found him, on the path leading down the mountain slope into the jungle that lay between the foothills and the sea. It was hot work, even under the shade of the overhanging trees. Though she was in a hurry to get it done and return to hiding, she had to stop from time to time and rest. She put the shovel down beside the rifle and sat on a fallen log, filling her lungs with the cooling downdraft from the top of the mountain range high above. Taking off her bush hat, she mopped her face, neck, and arms, and avoided looking at the body of her husband sprawled beside the hole she was digging.

Ferguson was exceptionally tall, and the blanket she'd brought down with the shovel couldn't cover all of him. It concealed his face, and came down to his thighs. His thin, hard-muscled legs stuck out, the feet bare. The men who'd killed him had requisitioned his boots and socks.

The rest period Nora allowed herself was brief. When her breathing returned to normal, she took up the shovel and resumed digging. She was a strong, resilient woman, not given to breaking down. A tall woman in her mid-thirties, with a good, buxom figure, she wore hiking boots, slacks, and a man's shirt. Her face was also strong; too strong to be pretty, but very pleasing to look at. There was no gray in her rich brown hair; and the few lines in her face had been put there by an easy-going, sensual enjoyment of life.

Comfortable, Ferguson had called her. Though he'd said it in bed, he hadn't meant only the soft warmth of her body. She was a woman who gave to a man, in many ways, and knew how to get what she wanted in turn without riling him. Through her, Ferguson had known unexpected pleasure and contentment in his last years.

He had come to mean a great deal to her; but she didn't let herself sink into grief or despair as she dug his grave. She had cried when she'd found him dead. Now there was the rest of her life to be considered; a new life to be sought for and grasped.

That was Nora's way, sustained by a tough-minded resilience and stubborn practicality. She was used to shutting doors on the past and starting over again. She'd been doing it since she was sixteen.

That was the year she'd left her divorced mother and worked her way across the country from Baltimore to Los Angeles to live with her father. They'd lived together for three years; good years that lasted until she was nineteen and got married to a young business administration graduate from UCLA. Her first husband's job had taken them to Hawaii, and it was there that their daughter had been born, and then their son. It was two years after the birth of their boy that her first husband had gotten himself killed in a car crash, driving home one night with too much liquor in him after an office Christmas party.

He'd left her with a mortgaged house and other debts she couldn't pay; and very little in the bank. She'd moved herself and the two kids into a small apartment and gotten a job as a barmaid in downtown Honolulu to support them.

She was thirty-one when Ferguson came into the bar one night, took a look at her, and stayed till closing, nursing beers and talking with her whenever she was free of other customers. Ferguson was in his late fifties, a widower without children who managed a rubber plantation far away on the island of New Britain. A lonely life.

Ferguson came into the place three nights running before he worked up the nerve to ask her out. He was in Honolulu on a one-week holiday. It got stretched to two weeks, and on the last day they were married. Nora and the children returned with him to New Britain.

The wild passion of her first marriage wasn't there, but Nora liked the quality of the man; and his need drew on her tenderness. Both the liking and the tenderness grew with their time together. Ferguson was good to her, good to her children. And the kids came to idolize him and relish the adventure of life on an isolated plantation. But their education suffered; so when they were old enough they were sent to private school in Australia, which was near enough for frequent visits back and forth by plane.

When the war with the Japanese hit the Pacific, Ferguson wanted to send Nora to Australia. She refused to go. Her children were safe, her husband needed her, and she didn't like being without a man. Ferguson didn't insist. In the beginning no one conceived that the enemy could possibly get this far south. When they did, with unbelievable swiftness, Nora and Ferguson were among the thousands caught by surprise inside the trap.

With Rabaul taken and the invading troops seizing positions around the coasts of the big island, Ferguson escaped from the plantation with her, slipped through the enemy net, and got her to a camouflaged coastwatcher shack hidden in the mountains overlooking the southwest coast.

The shack had sleeping and cooking facilities, a good supply of tinned food, and a Model 3B Teleradio capable of communicating with Coastwatcher Control in Port Moresby, on the southeast coast of New Guinea. It was part of the network of hidden radios throughout the chain of islands north of Australia. This one had been set up for

Ferguson two years earlier, when the war with Germany began, against the possibility of that war spreading this far.

The coastwatcher shack became their new home. At least once every day Ferguson radioed in reports of enemy planes overhead. Less often, there were enemy ships in the sea below to tell Control about. For a time it seemed they would be quite safe there, until the inevitable Allied counterattack freed them. But it didn't come. Instead, one day while he was scanning with his field glasses, Ferguson saw a small enemy patrol in the jungle below their hideout.

That decided him. He headed down to a native fishing village to find some kind of boat with which he could get Nora away. Once that was done, he'd intended to return to his job as coastwatcher on the enemy-held island. He was that kind of man. Had been.

When he didn't return by the following dawn, Nora headed down the mountains after him. And found him, sprawled dead beside the path.

Judging by the bullet wounds down his thin back, he'd been surprised by enemy soldiers on patrol and hit by a submachine gun burst as he fled. . . .

The grave was ready now; not as deep as she would have liked, but long enough to take his tall frame without bending the legs. Setting her jaw, she rolled his stiffened body into the trench she'd dug. Straightening, she took off her bush hat and stood silent for a minute; not praying, just saying goodbye to him. Then she began shoveling the dirt back in the hole, covering him.

It was dark when she got back to the coastwatcher shack. She radioed Port Moresby and let Control know what had happened. Until they could find a way to evacuate her, she would remain there and send in reports as her husband had done. When she signed off, she stretched out on the army cot in the shack's single room and fell asleep, too exhausted to eat or undress.

In the days that followed she waited, and radioed information on enemy air and sea movements. She was all alone now, and that was the one thing she'd always found it hard to handle. There wasn't much to do but think, and something was troubling her beside the loneliness. A week passed before she decided what it was: Ferguson's grave. He should have a headstone; or at least some kind of marker, until he could have a proper funeral.

Finding a plank of wood, Nora set to work with a knife. She carefully cut his name on it; and the dates of his birth and death. Then she carried it down to where she'd buried him.

It was on the way back that she found Sam Flood.

He awoke on the army cot and stared up at the palm-thatch ceiling, wondering where he was.

It was the first time he'd come all the way out of it since the malaria had gripped him in that swamp. But he could remember bits and snatches of things embedded in the fog of the fever that was now abating: water, first; trickling into his throat and strangling him, until he coughed his throat clear and began to drink greedily. The canteen being pulled away from him, forcibly. That had brought his eyes open, and he'd gotten a blurred look at the woman crouching beside him.

She'd pushed a couple pills between his chattering teeth, then let him have the water again to get them down. He remembered her talking. Asking him questions, he thought. He couldn't make out what she was saying. The words were sounds, nothing more. He couldn't connect up with them, couldn't remember any words of his own.

Walking. A lot of it, in short stretches, hanging onto her. And collapsing. A lot of that, too. Shaking and freezing with malaria. More pills.

Soup. When had she fed him hot soup?

It had been here, in the coastwatcher shack, but he didn't know that. Any more than he knew that it had taken her a day and a half to get him up here.

Suddenly the snatches of fever-ridden memory fled away from him as the important thing came rushing back at him from beyond the time of fever: There were twenty-one people in that enemy torpedo-boat base, waiting for him to get himself to Port Moresby and bring them help.

No. That was wrong. Only nineteen people now. Two were already dead. Killed because he had escaped.

Flood rolled on his side and shoved his legs off the cot, felt his bare feet thud to the plank flooring. Pushing with both hands, he sat himself up on the edge of the cot, fighting through waves of dizziness. When they subsided, he drew a deep breath and stood up. He fell with the first step, his rubbery legs giving way under his weight.

Nora came hurrying in and saw him on the floor, his face clenched like a fist in the effort he was exerting to get up on his hands and knees. He made it by the time she reached him. She got her hands under him and lifted. He concentrated on his legs, forcing them to do some of the work, to help her raise him enough to be dumped back on the cot.

As soon as he was on it he pushed up on one elbow, looking at her; really seeing her for the first time, studying her.

And then he was looking beyond her, his attention caught and held by what was behind her in the corner of the shack.

The coastwatcher radio equipment.

The
Mission

FIVE

With the war against Japan only months old, Michael Shaw had already suffered too many losses in too short a time for him to absorb.

He showed none of this as he worked out with his Unarmed Combat instructor on the field sixteen miles west of Brisbane, perspiring with exertion under the harsh sun. He looked very sound—a tall, rangy man of forty, with a lean, sunburned face and the purposeful sureness of manner to be expected of a captain in the Australian army. You had to search carefully in his dark gray eyes to find it: the weariness of the soul, the look of a man who has been inside hell.

His instructor was too young, and concentrating too much on his job, to be aware of it.

Shaw lunged for him, feinted a kick to the ankle, shifted and drove a forearm at the throat. He failed to make contact. His ankles were kicked out from under him and the hard ground came up and slammed his back, knocking the wind out of him. He tried a fast roll. It wasn't fast enough.

His instructor's heel came down on the side of his neck, just below the ear.

The heel only touched him, briefly; then was withdrawn, its point made. Shaw rose on one elbow in the dirt, sucking air back into his lungs, and looked up. His instructor's name was Neal Miller, and he was a corporal with the special commando group that had been shipped out from England to teach what they had learned. He was just eighteen, a compact, muscular lad with guileless blue eyes. There was still some plumpness to his handsome, pink-cheeked face; baby fat.

Miller grinned down at Shaw. "Almost caught me that time, sir."

A rush of liking for Miller flooded Shaw; an emotion stronger than liking. As soon as it came, Shaw realized why: Miller reminded him of the eldest of his two sons, Arthur.

Savagely, Shaw wiped that out of his mind. He jumped to his feet and attacked Corporal Neal Miller again, with a cold determination that was once more countered by the instructor's cool efficiency.

Except that the young commando called him "sir," and Shaw addressed him as "Miller," there was no rank between them out here on the field. They were merely two men engaged in mock battle; one very young and superbly trained, the other older and learning. Learning fast, so he could be among the first to strike back at an enemy that had inflicted that long list of personal losses on him. To strike back, and in striking perhaps diminish the agony of those nightmare memories.

The losses had begun to pile up, unbelievably, from the very start, with the Japanese invasion of Malaya. Captain Mike Shaw was in the forward defense system that crumbled with horrible swiftness before the onslaught of that horde of little men working their way through the jungle with their bicycles and guns. He became part of the unsteady retreat toward Singapore, watching the men he led dying around him as they fought a hopeless delaying action.

His losses began there and became uncountable: Ser-

geant Hawkins, Lieutenant Simms, Private Wells, Joe Par-
kin, Harry Rhoades— and all the ones whose names he'd
never known and never would know. Men who were his,
whether he knew their names or not. He'd led them, and
seen them die obeying him.

There weren't many left with him when the defense finally fell back on Singapore. A Singapore gone mad in his
absence, filled with the smoke and ruins of enemy bomb-
ing strikes, the massed confusion of people trying to get
out before the end, the crashing and ripping of prowling
bands of looters breaking into shops. The two greatest
British warships in the Pacific, the *Repulse* and the *Prince
of Wales,* had been sunk. The sea now belonged to the
enemy, along with the sky and the land. Singapore was
doomed.

Shaw had had close friends on both warships. All dead.
He made his way frantically through the confusion and
devastation of the city to his home. And felt no surprise at
what he found there. It was as though he'd already known
it; as part of the pattern. The house had taken a direct
bomb hit. With his wife and sons inside.

He moved through the last days of Singapore like a
sleepwalker. When he was ordered to leave, as one of the
officers who would be needed in Australia for the final defense or eventual counterattack, he made no objection.

The ship carrying them was sunk south of Java. An
enemy fighter plane strafed Shaw's lifeboat, ripping it
apart and killing everyone in it. Except Shaw. He floated
numbly in the ocean, buoyed up by his life jacket, and
watched the dead ones drift away from him: Major Davis,
Lieutenant Archer, Captain Rails, Captain Burton, a
nurse whose name he did not know. . . .

He floated limply for two days and two nights. When he
was picked up by another escape vessel, a tugboat, he was
unconscious. The tug was lucky, one of the few that got
through. But Shaw was not aware of the journey, or of
being carried ashore in Australia, or of being flown to the
hospital.

He was in the hospital for almost a week before he
began to be consciously aware again. And to remember . . .

Now, suddenly on that training field west of Brisbane, Shaw became aware of Corporal Neal Miller curled up in a ball at his feet, face contorted, clutching his middle with both hands. Shaw stared down at him, shocked.

Miller turned his head and looked up, his bared teeth clenched with ebbing pain.

"Sir," Miller gasped, "That was *too* much. You've got to hold back a bit, you know."

Shaw unfroze. "Sorry, Miller . . ." He reached down and took the boy's hand, helping him back onto his feet.

Miller braced his legs apart, still holding his middle and bending forward as he got his breath back.

"I really am sorry," Shaw apologized. "Bloody damn stupid of me."

Miller forced a rueful smile. "Happens, sometimes. You've got to remember all the time, sir, this is just practice. Save that stuff for the real thing."

Shaw nodded. That was what he needed: the real thing. And soon, or he'd go mad with all this pent-up hate. If he wasn't already.

The whistle blew across the field. Time for demolition instruction. Shaw rested a hand on Miller's burly shoulder briefly. Then he headed for the explosives bunker. As he trotted across the field, the image blinked on again inside his head, as vivid as ever: Amelia, Johnny, and Arthur, under the ruins of the house in Singapore. . . .

The image blinked off as he spotted Sergeant James hurrying toward him around the corner of the bunker. He slowed to a stop, waiting. The sergeant came to a ramrod halt and snapped a precisely correct salute.

"Sir. Colonel Manfred would like to see you in his quarters, sir. Immediately, sir."

Colonel Manfred leaned back in the swivel chair behind his desk and scratched a match into flame, carefully lighting his pipe as he squinted through the smoke at Shaw seated on the straight-backed chair opposite.

"Something interesting has turned up," he said as he flicked out the match. He dropped it in the ashtray on his desk. "Interesting, tricky, possibly a godsend but very much an odds-against. We've just got it from Port Moresby, which in turn got it this morning from a lady running one of their coastwatch radios on New Britain."

Shaw's surprise showed. "A woman coastwatcher?"

"Her husband was running the station. Plantation manager. Got himself killed, and his wife's stuck there." The colonel told him briefly about Sam Flood, and how Flood had gotten to Nora Ferguson with the information about the enemy torpedo-boat base. Then, in detail, he went into what he wanted Shaw to try to do about that base, and what Allied Command hoped from it if Shaw succeeded in pulling the mission off.

Shaw's eyes narrowed and his shoulders hunched forward just a bit.

Like a trained falcon straining at the leash, the colonel thought, studying him. He'd chosen the right man for this one. Maybe a little overtrained, or overbred. But that wouldn't hurt either, this time.

"You'll choose one man to go with you, Captain. One's all we can spare right now, I'm afraid. But if it can be done at all, that should be enough."

Shaw thought briefly, and nodded. "The main problem's going to be slipping inside at night to attach the explosives. The fewer men the more chance of that."

He didn't have to think about the man he wanted along with him. He'd already picked him.

Colonel Manfred found that his pipe had gone out. He struck another match and relighted it. Between puffs he said, "Captain, I'm sure it's as obvious to you as it is to me that your chances of getting away intact afterwards are pretty slim. To put it mildly. Even slimmer than the chances of accomplishing the mission in the first place."

"That's all right, sir."

"I thought it would be," the colonel said, carefully keeping his personal feeling about Shaw's eagerness to commit suicide out of his voice.

Shaw's shoulders hunched forward a bit more, his brain working quickly behind the intent, tormented eyes. "As you said earlier, sir, if putting this base out of action is going to be of any help to the people trapped north of there, I'll have to get it done soon. How do I get into New

Britain? Close enough to that woman's coastwatch station to make contact with the merchant seaman. I'll need him to give me the layout of the base."

"There'll be an army transport plane ready to fly you north in exactly two hours, Captain. To Port Moresby. That's as far as it can go without the certainty of running into enemy fighters. From Port Moresby, a Navy launch will be ready to nip you north around the corner to Buna."

"Why Buna? Why not all the way across to New Britain?"

"Because we've had a piece of luck. There just happens to be a man with a plane in Buna, who can get you there faster. And, we hope, put you down almost exactly where you want to go. It's not much of a plane. Not much of a man, either. But the right combination for this particular job."

Phil Qualey had spent his first night in Buna stealing the gasoline he needed. It wasn't too difficult to get away with. The small harbor town on the northeast coast of New Guinea was in too much of a barely controlled state of panic to pay much attention to the doings of one disreputable old bush pilot.

Qualey was a relic of the past; and Buna was preoccupied with its frightening present.

The Japanese had already occupied Lae and Salamaua, less than two hundred miles away along the coast. The invasion could engulf the Buna area any time the enemy wanted. There was no effective force to stop the invaders. Civilians were being evacuated as fast as vessels arrived to carry them around the eastern tip of New Guinea to the relative safety of Port Moresby.

As far as Qualey could see, he managed to pull off the theft without anybody noticing what he was up to. But it took most of the night, which didn't leave him enough time to transport the fifteen ten-gallon drums to the dock in secrecy. They would have to wait until the following night. So he hid the stolen gasoline in a fringe of jungle near the dirt road, and strolled back to his plane just before dawn.

The plane was moored next to a small dock where high overhanging trees concealed it from enemy observation planes that flew over almost every day. It was an old, weathered, much-patched little seaplane, with battered pontoons and a single nine-cylinder radial engine.

A relic, like himself.

On the nose of the plane, behind the propeller, its name was spelled out in fading, peeling blue paint: SKYLARK.

Qualey climbed into its cabin, and got a canteen from under his pilot's seat. It was filled with gin. There were two tied-down wicker chairs for passengers in the cabin. Behind these, in the section that was used to store gear, supplies, and spare gasoline, his sleeping bag was stretched out on the floor. He settled down on top of the bag, using it as a mattress, and soothed himself to sleep with the gin.

He woke in the early afternoon with a hangover and jittery nerves, both of which were soothed somewhat by a meal in town. Afterward, he spent the last of his cash buying rope and renting a work horse. Tethering the horse near the little dock, he climbed back inside the cabin of his plane and settled down in one of the wicker chairs to wait for dark. He spent the rest of the late afternoon gazing out at the Solomon Sea, steadily sipping gin and occasionally scratching his whiskers.

The whiskers itched, but he hated to shave. Partly, this was laziness. But it was also because he didn't like seeing what he'd become. The mirror insisted on showing Phil Qualey a crusty, deteriorating old bush pilot and prospector who'd been knocking around the islands of the southwest Pacific for twenty years without making anything of himself. That image bothered him.

Qualey preferred to go on thinking of himself as he'd been described in a 1929 *National Geographic* magazine article: "the ruggedly handsome, adventure-hunting, former World War ace." He'd torn the article out of the magazine, and still kept it folded in his wallet. There was a photograph of him in the article, fixing the *Skylark*'s engine: still a youngish man, wearing his World War I pilot's cap, with a thin mustache that set off a devilish grin.

That was how he thought of himself most of the time: as a tough, sharp young fella with a big future ahead, as soon as he finished sowing his wild oats.

The facts were that he was just about finished sowing oats; and that big future had been a mirage. He'd flown a lot of people in and out of otherwise inaccessible regions —miners, engineers, planters, oil men, prospectors, missionaries, anthropologists, photographers. All he'd earned from these jobs had gone into hunting a gold strike of his own; but he'd never dug up enough to buy more than a two-week spree in Darwin. The facts were that though still tough as a lean strip of time-worked leather, he was now as battered and weathered as his seaplane, with age and booze getting to him.

Those were the facts, but he didn't care to contemplate them close up any more than was absolutely necessary.

He preferred to contemplate the fact that he seemed to be running to luck right now. He'd been working a dig of his own deep in the interior of northern New Guinea when the war in the Pacific began. It was weeks before he'd learned of it, and by then the war was rushing south toward him.

He'd taken off and headed for civilization in short hops. Each place he stopped he managed to steal enough fuel to go a bit farther, not having the money to buy it. He was headed for the airfield at Lae, where he hoped to steal a full load of fuel, when one of his bouts of malaria forced him down in a jungle stream. That had been luck, too. If he'd reached Lae on schedule, he'd have been caught there in the enemy invasion.

When he recovered, he carefully circled the invaded area, flying by night. He'd landed here in Buna with the fuel indicator pointing to empty. Tonight, if his luck held, he'd finally have enough fuel in the tanks to make it south over the ridge to Port Moresby, where he could lift the gasoline for the last hop to Australia.

Only one thing could interfere with his luck now: Morison, Buna's civil administrator. There was bad blood between the two of them, from back in the days when Morison had been a patrol officer and had charged Phil Qualey,

twice, with smuggling. He'd squeaked free both times; but
it had been a near thing. . . .

By dark, Qualey had quite a bit of gin inside him. But
he was far from drunk. He remained wary as he led the
rented horse away from the dock area, carrying the coiled
rope across his shoulders. At the place where he'd hidden
the gasoline, he took his time, looking the situation over
until he was sure he was unobserved. Then he went into
the brush with the rope. Cutting a length, he tied one ten-
gallon drum to each end, and dragged them back to the
road.

He was slinging the first two drums on the back of the
horse when a flashlight blinked on, catching him dead in
the middle of its strong beam. Qualey turned to find Morison standing there, flanked by two sturdy native police
boys.

"I'm not stealing," Qualey blurted. "Just borrowing. I
figure to pay full value, soon's I raise the—"

"I agree you're not stealing," Morison broke in smugly.
"In wartime it's known as looting. The penalty is a good
deal more drastic."

Qualey tried to run. The native police boys caught him
before he'd gone fifty feet. With a look of deep-down satisfaction, Morison led the way to the town's small but very
solid jail.

The cell into which they put Qualey was small, with a
tiny window through which, if he craned his neck, he
could just catch a glimpse of the *Skylark* moored to the little dock. The sight of his plane waiting there to carry him
away was an added torment that became increasingly un-
bearable with the passing of time. With nothing else to do
but swat at flies, thirst for liquor, and curse the downturn
in his luck, he spent much of his time sleeping. He was
asleep when a fast naval yacht entered the harbor and
pulled up at the end of the dock where the Skylark was
moored.

Captain Shaw and Corporal Miller came off the yacht.
They were wearing jungle-camouflage battle dress. Each
had slung over his shoulder one of the Thompson subma-

chine guns just imported from America for special raiding force work. Each had a long commando knife and an Enfield Mark I revolver on his belt. Both carried big, bulky canvas bundles which they set down on the dock very carefully.

SIX

Morison came out onto the small dock alone to meet them as the naval yacht pulled away toward the harbor's main dock area, where a large group of refugees were waiting in the hot afternoon sun to cram themselves aboard for the return journey to Port Moresby.

Morison glanced at young Miller and shook hands briefly with Shaw as he introduced himself. "I'm Morison, Captain. Civil administrator." He looked nervously at the canvas bundles at their feet and lowered his voice. "Explosives?"

Shaw nodded. "Limpet mines and fuses. Plus an inflatable foldboat." He looked at the *Skylark*. "I take it this is the plane."

"Yes, but I wouldn't worry too much about the way it looks. It's still capable of flying you in there."

"I hope so." Shaw unslung his Thompson and gave it to Miller. "Get this stuff aboard. And stay with it."

"Yes, sir."

Shaw turned back to the civil administrator. "Where's the pilot?"

Morison's smile was just a trifle malicious. "Waiting. Though perhaps not too comfortably."

He led Shaw away from the dock as Miller began loading the canvas bundles into the plane.

When the native constable unlocked his cell, Qualey had just wakened from his late afternoon nap. He was lying on the hard, narrow bunk, squinting sourly at flies buzzing in a last patch of sunlight on the dirty ceiling above him. He didn't bother to turn his head when the constable came in.

"Get up. Mr. Morison wants you in his office."

That turned Qualey's head. He studied the constable's face, trying to judge from his expression the seriousness of the summons.

"What for?" Qualey did his best not to show the tremor of fear running through him.

The constable shrugged. "Not my business. Come on."

Qualey was slow about getting off the bunk. He knew damn well what the penalty was for looting in wartime. They *could* shoot you. But Morison wouldn't go that far, just because of an old grudge. Would he?

He toyed briefly with his chances of jumping the constable and getting that gun from his holster. Wisely he decided against it. The constable looked too young, tough, and ready for it.

His lower legs were shaky as he allowed himself to be conducted from the cell to Morison's office.

The constable withdrew after ushering Qualey into the administrator's office, shutting the door behind him. Morison was seated behind his desk. Shaw stood beside it at an at-ease stance that had nothing relaxed about it, his back to the windows, his hands linked behind him. The desk had been cleared of everything except a spread-out detail map of an area Qualey identified at a glance: the western portion of New Britain.

Qualey's eyes went back to Shaw, studying him with

worried suspicion. Shaw studied him in turn, sizing him up. Neither man was very much encouraged by what he saw.

"Qualey," Morison said, "this is Captain Shaw. I've just been telling him something of your rather colorful past. Including the two times you've been arrested on smuggling charges."

"Which you were never able to prove," Qualey reminded him with nasty relish. He just couldn't help it, in spite of his fear.

Morison's face darkened. Then he shrugged. "I'm willing to let bygones be bygones. What's important right now is that Captain Shaw needs your help." He looked at Shaw. "Captain, do you want to explain your mission to him?"

Qualey quickly decided there was no harm in trying: "I'm not much good at paying attention to things when I'm nervous." He held up his hands to let them see the way his fingers were trembling. "You've kept me locked up without a drop of liquor for three days."

Morison's angry response was cut short by Shaw's quiet: "Give him something to drink."

The civil administrator started to object, took a look at Shaw's face, and changed his mind. Reluctantly he got up and went to a corner cupboard.

Qualey looked gratefully at Shaw. They surely wouldn't be treating him like this if they intended to shoot him for looting, would they? But Shaw's expression was not reassuring. It was deadly earnest, businesslike, with no trace of any kindness or humor in it.

Morison returned and thumped a glass and a bottle of brandy on the desk. Qualey's eyes widened, his suspicion growing. It was good imported cognac, not local product. His feeling of suspicion did not prevent him from quickly opening the bottle and filling the glass. He drank down the whole glassful, gasped with pleasure, and refilled the glass. Holding onto both bottle and glass, he settled into a chair facing the desk and eyed the other two men.

thing pretty big, Captain."

"Damn good stuff. This mission of yours must be some-

Shaw gestured at the map on the desk. "I understand you know this area pretty well."

"Well as anybody. Flown in and out of there maybe forty times."

Shaw's forefinger went to a small X marked deep in the mountains. His forefinger moved to the nearest point on a wriggling line marked Snake River. "Do you know this river?"

Qualey nodded and sipped at the cognac. "But it ain't really a river. The Snake's just a narrow, twisty mountain creek."

"But not too narrow for a seaplane to land in?" Shaw asked.

"Depends. It'd have to be a small plane, like mine. I managed it once, a little farther down than where you're pointing. But it wasn't easy. The jungle grows in close on both sides. In places, the trees on the banks cover it completely. The man I flew in had to pay me double on account of . . ."

Qualey stopped himself. Suddenly he realized he could be talking himself right into trouble. His suspicions, which had been vague before, began to focus.

He took a hasty gulp of cognac. "Captain, suppose you tell me what this is all about?"

Shaw indicated the area of sea on the map above New Britain. "Up here we've got escape vessels packed with people waiting for a chance to slip through the Vitiaz Straits to Australia. They can't get through by day. Too many enemy planes patrolling the passage. And almost every ship that's tried to get through at night in the past week has been sunk. By torpedo boats operating out of an enemy base hidden here on the south coast, it turns out. Our first information about this base came from a seaman named Flood who escaped from it. It was radioed to us yesterday from a coastwatcher station—" his fingertip touched the X on the map "—being operated at the moment by a widow named Nora Ferguson. . . ."

Qualey was startled. "Widow? What happened to *Marty* Ferguson?"

Morison sat up straighter behind the desk. "You knew Ferguson?"

"Sure. Did a few jobs for him."

"He's dead. Seems the enemy spotted him, and he tried to run. They killed him."

"That's a real shame," Qualey said sincerely. "He was nice people. So's Mrs. Ferguson."

Morison seized on this: "That's one of the reasons we want you to fly Captain Shaw in there. To bring her out to safety."

Qualey was absolutely still for a long moment. Then he said softly: "Now hold on just a minute. What're you talking about? I can't do a thing like that."

"Why not?" Shaw snapped.

"Because my plane's on its last legs, that's why. It just won't fly that far nonstop anymore." He got as much sincerity as he could into his face and voice. "I'm sure sorry about Mrs. Ferguson, and I'd sure like to help if I could. But my plane just won't do it. If we tried, we'd just get dumped in the ocean halfway there."

Shaw's eyes were narrowed on him. "That doesn't square with my information."

"Well, Captain, your information is wrong. Dead wrong. I'm sorry. Real sorry."

Qualey raised his half-filled glass in a regretful toast. "Here's to poor old Ferguson. . . ." He drained the glass and immediately refilled it.

Morison started to say something, but Shaw stopped him by raising a hand, his eyes still fastened on Qualey.

"Mrs. Ferguson is only *one* of the people whose lives are at stake," he told him. "There are several thousand more, waiting to slip south through these straits. And time is running out on them. According to reports received by us, enemy warships are on their way to scoop up every Allied vessel in that area. This torpedo-boat base must be knocked out—so those escape vessels can make one final try to get through. Which will be exactly three nights from now."

"My prayers go with them," Qualey said, and drank a

silent toast to their hopes. He seemed, in fact, to be doing a lot more drinking than listening.

"That enemy base can't be hit by our planes," Shaw continued evenly. "They've got overwhelming air superiority. The few bombers we've got left wouldn't even get that far. So I've been sent, together with another man, to try to slip inside that base and get the job done with explosives. To do it, we've first got to be flown in and put down near Mrs. Ferguson's station—so we can reach her and Flood, the seaman."

Shaw paused for emphasis. "You are the only pilot handy who knows the interior well enough to get us in there at night—*tonight*. And your plane is the only one around slow enough and maneuverable enough to be able to set down in one of those narrow jungle streams. So, you're elected."

"Like hell I am. I told you, my plane's just too old to make that kind of trip."

"Whether it is or it isn't," Shaw told him flatly, "you're going to make the attempt. I've got no other choice. And neither do you."

"In a pig's eye I haven't!" Qualey emptied his glass and started to refill it again.

Morison snatched the bottle out of his trembling hand. "Qualey, Captain Shaw just told you: You have no choice. You don't. Believe me."

Qualey's temper flared, generated by terror, resentment, and liquor: "No! I won't do it. You can't make me do it. I'm not in the military, I'm a civilian and I don't have to take orders from anybody. The only mission I'm interested in is getting me and my plane to Australia before those Japs reach here."

"So," Shaw said softly, "your plane *can* make that distance, after all."

Qualey could have strangled himself. He sank into sullen silence, his face a mask of stubborn refusal.

Morison leaned toward him across the desk, evident pleasure in his voice: "I remind you that you are in jail on a serious charge. Looting in wartime. And this charge *will* stick. I'll have you in that jail cell a long time, Qualey. A matter of *years*. If the enemy comes this far, I'll *leave* you there; for them to find, along with that damned plane of yours."

Qualey stared at Morison. "That's blackmail. . . ."

Morison smiled. "Purely and simply."

Qualey's resistance crumpled. He looked to Shaw.

"He means it," Shaw told him thinly. "So do *I*."

Miserable, Qualey gave in ungraciously to the inevitable. He groaned and closed his eyes. When he opened them, Shaw's stare was still fastened to his face. Quickly, Qualey shifted his eyes to Morison.

"I need gasoline. Enough to fill the tanks, and refuel for the return trip . . . if there ever is one."

Morison got a slip of paper from his desk and wrote on it. "Here you are. This is a chit for whatever amount of fuel you'll need. Plus transport."

Qualey's face was bitter as he took it and stood up. "Can I go now?"

Morison called out to the native constable, who reentered immediately. "Mr. Qualey is free to leave. Pass the word."

Qualey hurried out, smiling slyly to himself as soon as his back was turned to them.

When he was gone, Morison looked thoughtfully at Shaw. "Better get down there, Captain. I don't think he'd run off without his plane. It means too much to him. But once he has it fueled—he *could* just get in and fly off."

Shaw smiled for the first time, a smile that did not soften the bleak lines of his face.

"Not likely . . ."

The army lorry carrying Qualey and the fuel pulled up to the small dock an hour before dusk. Qualey climbed out eagerly, and a soldier in back began handing down the drums of gasoline to him. As the last drum was set down and the lorry pulled away, Qualey turned to look at the *Skylark*. He was jolted by the sight of someone inside it.

Thinking quickly, he crossed the dock and opened the

cabin door. He looked in at Corporal Miller sitting in one of the wicker chairs, looking back at him with those mild blue eyes. Qualey took in the camouflage battle dress, the gun and knife on his belt. "You're the fella doing this job with Captain Shaw, right?"

"Yes. You're the pilot?"

"Uh-huh. The captain wants you in the civil administration office, on the double."

"Captain Shaw ordered me to stay here until he gets back."

"Well he just changed the orders," Qualey snapped, desperation plucking at him. "Asked me to tell you to come up there. Got some last minute problem to talk over with you."

"I'm sorry, sir," Miller told him politely, "but I'd have to hear that change in orders from the captain himself, personally."

Qualey's control broke. "Get off my plane, dammit! I've got to take her over to the main dock for some repairs, in a hurry."

Miller reached down a hand between the big canvas bundles behind him, and brought up one of the submachine guns. He placed it casually across his knees, not exactly pointing at Qualey. "I'm sorry, sir."

Qualey glared at him. Then he carefully rearranged his face into a careless grin. "What the hell, no skin off my ass if you don't want to carry out his orders. That's your business."

He climbed into the plane, went past Miller in a crouch to his sleeping bag. Getting the canteen from inside it, he shook it experimentally and listened to the sloshing inside. About half full. He unscrewed the cap to give Miller a whiff of the gin inside.

"Drink?" He held out the canteen. "It's good gin. The best."

The corporal shook his head. "I don't drink, sir."

Qualey sighed, his last hope gone. "Well I do." He tipped the canteen to his mouth and took a long swallow.

Then he took another look at Miller and gave up.

Screwing the cap back on, he dropped the canteen on the sleeping bag and started out.

"Come on," he said wearily, "you can help me with the fuel. Then we'd better scrub the barnacles and seaweed off the bottoms of the pontoons so they won't drag."

SEVEN

Dusk was closing in on Buna when Qualey cast off the mooring lines. After one last check on the strengthening breeze pouring off the land to the sea, he climbed into the cabin of his plane and shut the door. It was already murky inside. The faces of Shaw and Miller, strapped into their wicker chairs, were becoming blurs. He sat down at the controls and flicked on the instrument panel light; there'd be no others turned on this trip. He glanced at the horizon indicator and compass. They seemed to be working. The altimeter had quit on him long ago.

The *Skylark* began to bob and roll in the shore swells, water slapping aainst the pontoons, the fuselage creaking.

"Hold on," he said without looking back over his shoulder. "Wind's from the shore in the evening. I'm going to have to taxi out a stretch and turn back into it for take-off."

"You're in charge here," Shaw's voice conceded unemotionally.

"That you don't have to tell me." With his hands on the controls, he no longer felt helpless and humiliated. *They* were helpless now; their lives and fate up to him. It felt good; it always felt good.

His fingers curled around the rough, worn rubber grip and moved the stick experimentally. His feet tested the rudders. Everything responded normally. His free hand reached for the throttle and opened it just enough, went to the ignition and switched on.

The engine coughed and caught with a sputtering roar. The propeller jerked into movement, kicking over once, twice, and then going into a continuous whirl. The *Skylark* taxied downwind away from the shore, the wire struts vibrating with strain as the wings shoved the air, their tips dipping from side to side as the plane lurched sluggishly through the waves.

The plane began to bounce forward as the pontoons hit the waves with increasing force, slamming through them, smashing spray up over the wings. Qualey opened up the throttle, and the plane surged forward faster. He made a rough estimate, based on the approximate force of the shore wind and the weight being carried by the plane. When he judged they were far enough out for a takeoff he eased up on the throttle, swinging her back toward the shore. The *Skylark* made the turn clumsily, wallowing.

Then he opened up again, and the *Skylark* was rushing into the wind, the engine revving up deafeningly. The ancient fuselage vibrated alarmingly. The high outspread wings caught at the air, lifting the plane, the pontoons riding higher in the water now. Their bottoms smacked the wavetops, throwing up walls of spray on either side of the cabin.

And then, quite suddenly, the spray was below them. The blasting roar of the hard-laboring engine became a steady, purring growl. The plane stopped rocking like a cork as it entered its natural element, climbing skyward smoothly through the darkening air.

Qualey dipped a wing and banked into a slow turn away from the land. He flattened out as the *Skylark* winged northward, keeping it low over the sea to lessen the chances of being spotted by enemy fighters.

It was night when they sighted the coast of New Britain. The moon was almost full and the sky relatively unclouded, showing clearly the white line of surf below and the dark looming bulks of the mountains ahead. Drawing on his memory of years of flying the area, Qualey studied the different shapes of the mountains as he left the sea behind. Spotting his landmarks, he banked towards one of the highest mountains, its top shrouded by a patch of small fluffy grey clouds.

Miller's voice sounded sharply in back of him: "There's a plane. Off to the left."

A fist squeezed Qualey's heart. He jerked his head around at the same time as Shaw.

It was a plane all right; an enemy fighter by the speed of it, streaking north over the mountains of the interior.

It was far away, but if they could spot it, it could spot them.

Qualey jerked his head forward again as he quickly throttled down as far as he dared, praying she wouldn't stall on him. The *Skylark* dropped like a rock toward the protective darkness of the land below. At the last second Qualey opened up on the throttle a bit. The plane skimmed over the jungle, the pontoons just missing the highest treetops. Qualey concentrated on the dark ground ahead.

"Tell me what it's doing!" he snarled. "I can't look."

"It hasn't changed course," Shaw told him tightly. "I don't think it saw us. Looks like one of their Zeros. Probably heading back to its home base for the night."

A hill suddenly materialized, dead ahead. Qualey grunted and his right hand jerked the stick back between his knees while his left opened the throttle all the way. The *Skylark* bounced upward. The pontoons barely managed to clear the trees on the hilltop. Qualey leveled out, keeping low, but not quite as low as before.

"It's gone," Shaw said behind him a moment later. "We're safe."

"Anything *else* around?"

There was a silence as the men behind him looked around.

"No. Not at the moment at any rate."

Qualey headed up to a reasonable height. He let his breath out slowly, drew a few more before he could speak again. "Night flying at low altitude ain't recommended for heart conditions."

Shaw was startled. "You have a heart condition?"

"If I don't *now,* I never will."

Qualey located the cloud-topped mountain again and banked toward it, aiming between two lower mountains. The plane dropped suddenly as it hit a downdraft from the valley below. Qualey opened up the throttle. The rickety old plane shuddered and rocked, then bucked upward again, bouncing on the bumpy air.

Qualey waited until they were beyond the valley into calmer air, and the *Skylark* was behaving itself again. Then he peered downward, searching. Finally he saw what he was looking for: the moonlit glint of a stream twisting through the high jungle below. He banked toward it, pointing with his left hand.

"There it is. Snake River. I think."

"We have to be *sure,*" Shaw growled at him.

"No way we can get any surer, at night. I *think* that's it. That's the best I can do."

Shaw repressed a flare of anger, admitting to himself reluctantly that the man couldn't give more than he had to give. The best they could do was all any of them could give.

"Remember," he said, "we want to set down close to that coastwatcher station."

"I'll get you as close as I can. *How* close, depends on the way the land lies, not me. Now just shut up and let me concentrate on not cracking us up."

Qualey began to circle down, slowing as he did so, bringing down the engine roar until he could hear the wind shrieking as it tugged at the shuddering wingstruts. The *Skylark* plunged down into the darkness. He snapped off the instrument panel light so he could see out better.

Reaching down with his left hand, he pushed at the top of a rod he had installed in the plane himself many years back. It went right through the floor of the fuselage, and fully extended the bottom of the rod was exactly two feet below the pontoons. It was a system invented back around 1930 by pilots making the first night landings on water. Qualey still used it.

When it was all the way down, he hooked the top of the rod behind his right leg. He could feel the vibration of the wind biting at it as he tried to relocate the stream from the lower altitude, flying only a couple hundred feet above the dense jungle.

When he spotted it again, he circled to below what he judged to be the spot corresponding with the *X* on Captain Shaw's map. Then he swung upstream. Landing against the current, he'd have to cover a shorter distance before bringing the *Skylark* to a stop; which would lessen the chances of smashing against something, or going over a waterfall, or into a stretch of rapids.

Flying as low and slow as he dared, he hunched forward and concentrated on the stream below. In places, it disappeared entirely where the trees on the banks overhung it. In others it was clear, but making too many sharp turns. He followed the turns, searching. Finally he saw what he needed ahead: a straight stretch of stream that was long enough.

Holding his breath, he lined the plane up with it and brought it slowly down, a bit at a time. Abruptly, the jungle was rushing past on either side of the plane. They were almost down. Qualey slowed the plane a bit more, bringing it lower; praying and concentrating at the same time on not hooking a wingtip into the trees on the banks of the stream.

Then he felt what he was waiting for: the top of the rod jerked hard against the back of his leg as the bottom of it dipped into the water. He cut the engine. The *Skylark* dropped the rest of the way, hitting the stream with a great splash. Qualey fought to keep the plane going straight upstream as it slowed, settling into the water.

It had almost come to a halt when the left pontoon

struck a submerged rock with a jarring wrench. The sounds of crunching and splintering knifed straight to Qualey's heart. He groaned aloud as the *Skylark* drifted sideway to the right bank of the stream. It came to a stop in the mud.

Cursing savagely, Qualey jumped out with Shaw and Miller. Pulling at the mooring ropes, they dragged the wounded plane up onto the stream bank as far as they could, where it would be hidden from air observation by the overhanging jungle foilage. Then, while Shaw and Miller dragged their gear out of the plane, Qualey unhappily examined the smashed pontoon.

The front of it was caved in. But its supports still seemed undamaged.

"I can fix it," Qualey announced. "Take me a couple days maybe. I'll work on it while you're off doing your job. That way it'll be ready to fly us out when you get back."

But Shaw knew better than to trust him to wait here for them. "You're going with us. We can repair the damage *after* the mission. Come over here."

His tone left no room for argument. The disgruntled Qualey trudged over to the other two men. Shaw had spread his map out on the ground and was shining a small light on it. He touched the *X*.

"Where are we in relation to the coastwatcher station? Exactly."

"I don't know, *exactly*," Qualey got a certain amount of unreasonable satisfaction out of that. He moved a finger along a stretch of the Snake River representing a few miles. "Somewhere along here, I reckon."

"That's not good enough," Shaw snapped.

"It's the best I can do," Qualey told him sourly. "You're the big military leader. You figure out where we are."

Shaw studied the land around them. But it was too dark to identify any landmarks corresponding with the map. "No sense blundering around looking for it blindly," he decided reluctantly. "We'll have to wait here till dawn."

As it turned out, they only waited about an hour. Miller was the first to hear something. He snatched up his submachine gun, looking at Shaw.

Shaw listened, then nodded. Someone was coming through the jungle toward them. Motioning for Qualey to stay down and keep still, he gestured at Miller. The corporal melted into the dark jungle to the right. Shaw moved off to the left, to a thick tree trunk, taking his Thompson with him. He raised the submachine gun as two figures emerged from the bushes, each carrying a rifle. He lowered it when he saw one of them was a woman.

He stepped away from the tree trunk so they could see him "Mrs. Ferguson?"

They came to an abrupt halt, staring at him in the jungle-shadowed moonlight.

"Yes," she said, after a moment's hesitation.

"I'm Captain Shaw." He pointed to Miller coming out of the bushes and Qualey rising from the ground. "Corporal Miller; and I believe you know Mr. Qualey, our pilot." He looked at the man with Nora Ferguson. "You're Sam Flood."

Flood nodded. He looked gaunt in spite of his stocky build. Fever had melted the flesh from him, leaving the skin stretched too taut over the solid bones of his face and body. But at least he could walk under his own steam again. He looked disgustedly at Shaw, Miller, and Qualey.

"Three? That's all they sent to hit that Jap base?"

"No," Qualey corrected him, and pointed to Shaw and Miller. *"Two.* I'm just along as a driver. I flew us in, and I'll fly us out. If any of us're left afterwards. Which I doubt."

"We're all they could spare," Shaw told Flood. "Anyway, we couldn't have gotten many more in that plane. The limpet mines we've brought along will have to make up the difference." He turned to Nora Ferguson. "Is your place far?"

"No. We heard the plane, and thought it might be you."

Shaw frowned. "Any enemy troops close enough to have heard us too?"

"I don't think so. There've been some patrols in this area, but I think they go back to their camps at night. I can't be certain though."

Shaw decided they'd have to take their chances. "All right, let's get going."

With Qualey forced to help carry the canvas bundles, they headed for the coastwatcher shack.

As they trudged along following Flood, Qualey offered Nora his sympathy on the death of her husband. She accepted his condolences with a calm self-possession that made Shaw look at her sharply.

"You take it remarkably well, Mrs. Ferguson." Shaw meant it as a compliment, but it came out too tight.

Nora Ferguson looked at Shaw for a long moment, recognizing the withdrawn, too-controlled manner of the man. The kind of man she was good with, because she knew how to relax those controls.

"My husband was a good man," she said finally. "But he is dead. If I keep dwelling on that, I won't have anything left for the living. I've got myself and two children to think of now."

"I see." Shaw was silent for a time. Then he asked, "Where are your children?"

"Safe in Australia, thank God."

"You're lucky. We'll try our best to get you to them, Mrs. Ferguson. As soon as we've accomplished this mission."

She nodded, and looked at him again. "Are you married, Captain?"

"My wife was killed in Singapore." He tried to speak as calmly as she had, but it still came out too tight.

"Children?"

"They're dead too."

She didn't say anything to that. Too many people were dying lately to keep saying you were sorry.

But she looked at him thoughtfully from time to time, as they continued up the slope to the coastwatcher shack.

"The way Nora and me have figured it, this must be where the base is." Flood pointed to the mouth of a river on the map spread out on the table. "That fits the time it took me to get from there to where she found me. And it's the only river that size along that stretch of coast."

Flood, Shaw, and Miller stood around the table, looking at the map in the light of a small lantern. Qualey was helping Nora to get tea ready.

Shaw studied the area between where they were and the location of the enemy base. "Mrs. Ferguson, would you come over here a moment."

When she came over, he pointed to the map. "What is our shortest and safest route from here? Short enough to get us there tomorrow night. Safe enough so we're not too likely to walk smack into the enemy along the way."

Her finger traced a route. "This is your best way. Sticking to the highlands down to the river, and then down the river."

"Can we make that in time?"

"Less, if you don't run into trouble or get lost. There's a dirt road part of the way, here. But that would be too dangerous. Better stick to the brush north of the road. The trouble is, there are trails through the jungle there, but it's easy to wander off along the wrong ones if you don't know them." She thought about it. "I'd better go along, to show you the way."

Shaw gave it some scowling thought too. "I'm afraid we'll have to take you up on that, Mrs. Ferguson. At least to the river. From there we can't get lost. Once we reach it you can turn back and wait for us here."

"What about me?" Qualey demanded.

"I'll decide that when we get there," Shaw told him. "Depends partly on whether you've behaved yourself." He looked to Flood. "Now I'd like you to draw the layout of the base for me, as accurately as you can remember."

"I already have." Flood got a folded sheet of paper from his pocket and opened it on the table. One by one he explained what his marks meant: the river, the dock, the positions of the tanker, the stranded hulk, the four torpedo boats when they were docked during the day, the lookout tower with its machine gun, the guard positions, the Japanese commander's bungalow, the two personnel shelters that had already been built, and the positions where more had been intended, plus the locations of the latrines he'd help dig.

"You've got a good memory for details," Shaw congratulated him, studying the layout.

"That's the way it *was*. They may have changed some of it since I escaped. Especially the guard setups."

"How about patrols in the area around the camp?"

"They've got two of them prowling the interior on either side of the river all day. Four men each."

"What about at night?"

"I don't know. I was shut up inside the hull of this grounded ship all night."

"How big a garrison have they got? Roughly."

"Exactly twenty-four men, including troopers and maintenance men. Plus the crews of the torpedo boats, by day. Each of them has an eleven-man crew, so that makes forty-four more."

Shaw looked at Flood with surprised respect. "Well, now we know what we're up against." He scowled down at the layout. "About as bad as we expected, Miller. You can see our chances of getting inside this base undetected, even by night, are pretty slim."

"It does look that way, sir," the corporal agreed. But if that worried him a great deal, he didn't show it.

"But we're still going to have to try. If we do get in, we'll concentrate on attaching the mines to this tanker, here. With the fuses set to go off when the torpedo boats are at dock beside it. If we can, we'll also stick some mines to the underside of the dock itself. But when that tanker blows up, it should take all four MTBs with it."

Flood was eyeing Shaw, not liking the direction the discussion was taking. "Wait a minute. Let's talk about the problem of getting the prisoners out of there first."

Shaw looked at him grimly. "We'll try to get them out, *after* we achieve the main objective: blowing up the base and those torpedo boats. Be a lot easier then, in the confusion. . . ."

"If any of them are left alive! Those explosions could

kill a lot of them. If the men are still inside that hulk when the tanker goes off, they'll *all* be killed."

"I'm aware of that danger." Shaw's voice was low, but steady. "But dangers of that kind can't be avoided in a war area."

Flood brushed that aside as meaningless. "We've *got* to get them out before you blow up the base. I'm responsible for them being prisoners. Two of them were executed for my escape."

"I'm sorry. But your problems with your conscience can't be allowed to wreck a military operation of this importance. I've got conscience problems of my own I had to learn to live with."

He didn't go into the details of all the people who had died following him in defeat. Nor did he say aloud that at last he had a chance of striking back at the enemy, and Flood's conscience wasn't going to be allowed to interfere with that.

"Listen," Flood told him desperately, "I've already figured out a way to knock out that base by freeing the prisoners first, and using their help."

Shaw shook his head. "I can think of more ways than you. But all of them cut our already slim chance of success even slimmer."

"If you kill those prisoners blowing up that base, you'll be *murdering* them!"

Shaw stiffened. But his voice remained low, rigidly controlled. "If that's the name you want to put to it, so be it. It's my responsibility."

"I don't care whose responsibility it is!" Flood snarled at him.

"Flood, try to think of the number of people involved, and you'll understand the situation. There are only nineteen prisoners inside this base. There are several *thousand* on those escape vessels, waiting to slip through the straits three nights from now. The lives of those thousands depend on our blowing up the base and those torpedo boats."

But Flood was viciously impatient with this juggling of

numbers against numbers: "I don't *know* any of those thousands. I do know these prisoners you're ready to sacrifice."

Shaw forced himself to look directly into the angry eyes of the other man and made a last try at making him understand: "There's no point in arguing, Flood. It's not my choice to make. I'm under *orders*."

"Orders to wipe out that base, not to kill our own people."

Shaw was silent for a long moment. Then he said, "All right. We'll see, after we're inside the base, if the prisoners can be rescued without endangering the objective of this mission. *If* they can, naturally I'll be as happy as anyone."

Flood knew Shaw was only placating him. But he forced himself to stop, seeing that talk wasn't going to sway this man. His eyes narrowed, got a hooded look.

"Yeah," he said slowly, in a tone that could mean anything, "we'll have to do that—see what can be done when the time comes."

Nora spoke up quietly, her voice breaking the confrontation: "Tea's ready. . . ."

They bedded down early that night, Nora on the bunk and the men on the floor. Flood lay in the dark with his hands under his head, thinking his own private thoughts. All of them involved the nineteen people held prisoner in the enemy base. Finally, he focused on just one of them: Esther, the Filipino nurse.

He let himself think about Esther for some time. Then he went to sleep.

III

The
Trek

EIGHT

They set out with the first light of dawn, a last hot breakfast inside them. The explosives had been divided between Shaw and Miller, in canvas bundles fitted with loops to go over the shoulders, so they could be carried on their backs like knapsacks. In a similar arrangement, Flood carried the inflatable foldboat that would take them down the river to the enemy base. Nora and Qualey had the food and extra ammunition, and they all had water canteens. Each of the four was armed; Shaw and Miller with the submachine guns and the weapons in their belts, Flood and Qualey with the rifles that had belonged to Nora and Ferguson; Nora with an old .45 automatic her husband had left behind.

Shaw led the way, his eyes and ears alert for any sign of an enemy presence. Nora hiked beside him, guiding them along the shortest safe routes down the mountains and through the jungle to the river. Qualey and Flood followed, in that order. Corporal Miller moved freely on roving patrol, sometimes scouting ahead or dropping behind, other times disappearing into the jungle on either side for a time.

It was hard going, over rugged broken ground in steaming heat, and from the start Shaw set a brisk, determined pace. Within an hour, Qualey was gumbling.

"I'm an old man. And I ain't a fighting man. And you got no business dragging me along on something as rough as this, damn you!"

Shaw ignored him, and looked inquiringly at the sweat-streaked woman trudging along beside him.

"Don't worry," she quietly reassured him, "I'm all right. I'm strong enough to handle a hike like this. And anything else I have to handle."

Her smile, and the warmth and reaching out for contact that was in it, startled him.

So did his grin.

"Good girl."

An unspoken sense of understanding had begun between them; knowingly offered by Nora, and hungrily seized upon by the lonely, tormented Shaw.

They were following a well-worn path through a thick-forested mountain slope when Miller, who had vanished around a bend up ahead, came back on the double.

His voice was just enough above a whisper to be heard by them all: "Enemy patrol. Coming this way."

"How many?" Shaw was already motioning the others into the dense jungle to the right of the path. He had warned them before starting out about such a possibility, and about leaving as little sign of their going as possible.

"Ten or eleven."

They followed the others into the thick foliage, crouching carefully so they wouldn't break any branches and give themselves away. When they were deep enough in to be hidden, Shaw motioned Nora behind a rock, Flood and Qualey behind a fallen, rotting tree. They obeyed quickly, each holding a weapon ready.

"Keep still and don't shoot unless I start it." Shaw unslung his Thompson, got it ready. "I won't, unless they spot us."

He went to one knee with the stock of the submachine

gun held hard to his shoulder, sighting along it through a tangle of vines. Miller had faded to his left and became almost invisible merely by standing absolutely motionless in the shadow of a tree.

Shaw heard the enemy patrol before he could see it. When he could see them, it was only flickering glimpses through the dense foliage. Holding his breath, he watched with his finger taut across the trigger, slippery with sweat. He counted each enemy trooper as he went past. Miller had been right. There were eleven of them.

They didn't pause at the place where Shaw and the others had left the path.

Shaw listened to the sounds of their going, up the path into the mountains. When he could no longer hear them, he waited another full minute before motioning to Miller. The corporal moved out of the shadow of the tree, toward the path.

Moments later he called softly: "It's all right. They're gone."

Only when Shaw let out his breath did he realize how tightly he'd been holding down the fear, and the lust to kill. He rose to his feet.

"All right," he said shakily, "let's get out of here."

Qualey got up looking even more worried than before. "The way they're headed, they could stumble on my plane. Let me get back to it."

"No."

"If they find it, they *wreck* it. . . ."

"Shut up." Shaw said it quietly, but Qualey looked at his eyes and fell back a step, frightened.

They moved back to the path and continued along it in the direction of the river.

Shortly after noon they reached a high mountain ledge that gave them a dizzying view of the foothills and jungle spread out below to the sea.

Nora moved to the edge and pointed down. "That's it. Your river."

Shaw and the others moved over beside her and looked down. From the ledge under their feet a cliff dropped away almost sheer to the down-rushing waters of a river far below. Shaw raised his eyes to take in the vast stretch of jungle and swamp that hid the continuation of the river where it reached to the sea. Hidden somewhere in there, too, was the enemy base he was going to do everything in his power to destroy.

Taking the provisions from Nora, he put them down.

She stretched and arched her shoulders, gratefully. "Thanks. I *am* a little tired."

"We'll take an hour's rest and eat here."

"Not me," Flood said. "Not here at the edge. Heights make me nervous." He took Qualey's arm and led him away from the edge. "You and me can eat here, where its nice and safe."

Qualey grinned at him crookedly, shrugged, and settled down to open the provisions he'd been carrying.

Shaw unslung the big canvas bundle he'd been toting and put it down carefully. "Stick with the explosives," he told Miller quietly.

Miller nodded. He put his own bundle of explosives down beside it. Shaw picked up the provisions Nora had been carrying and moved away along the top of the cliff with them. Nora followed, sensing that he wanted to be with her, a bit away from the others.

He stopped again at the edge, looking down. The river was wild below, the water plunging down at great speed from the mountains in a series of short waterfalls and violent rapids.

"You can't get down directly from here," Nora told him. "You'd have to go further up in the mountains and work your way back down. Take a couple days."

Shaw shook his head. "This stretch won't do, anyway. What we need is water calm enough to use the foldboat."

"That's down below, where the river levels off." As she sat down, Nora pointed off to where the river vanished under jungle and did not reappear.

Shaw gazed in that direction for a time, then glanced at the others. Approvingly, he saw that Corporal Miller, having gotten his meal from Qualey, had gone back to eat it sitting by himself beside the two canvas bundles of explosives. Lowering himself to the ground with Nora, he helped her get out their midday meal.

Flood, sitting on the ground with his back toward Miller, was eating slowly and mechanically, his eyes fastened on Qualey. He spoke between mouthfuls, his voice low, for Qualey's ears only.

"How'd you like to get back to your plane? Right *now?* Instead of being dragged along on this and maybe getting yourself killed?"

Qualey swallowed a mouthful of food and looked at Flood with exaggerated weariness. "You kidding? That's all I want: to get me and my plane the hell out've here. Only that captain over there ain't gonna let me. That crazy son of a bitch."

Angrily, he forked more food in his mouth and chewed vigorously to let off steam. Flood put more food in his mouth and swallowed without chewing it, his eyes never leaving the pilot.

"He can't pull off his mission without those explosives," Flood said slowly. "He'd have to quit."

Qualey had no trouble getting the undertone of meaning. With another forkful poised halfway to his mouth, he looked at Flood with narrowing eyes, quietly absorbing the tempting thought. It was also coming to him that Flood was his kind of guy.

But a small finger of suspicion moved in Qualey. "I thought you were anxious to get down there and do something about them friends of yours that're prisoners there?"

"I'd rather have them be prisoners than dead. Doing what Captain Shaw wants, I'm just helping to kill them. And I'm not going to do it."

Qualey read how much Flood meant it in his eyes. He glanced over to where Corporal Miller was guarding the explosives, then met Flood's eyes again.

"All right, you sneaky bastard," he asked softly, "what've you got in mind?"

"We should get to that part of the river by late this afternoon," Nora was telling Shaw as she ate. "From there on, all you've got to do is stay with it."

Shaw nodded abstractedly, looking at the jungle spread out far below, listening to the faint sounds of the river rising up to him. "You'll turn back when we reach it. Wait for us at the coastwatcher station." His pause was barely perceptible. "If we don't join you sometime during the following day, it will be because we can't. Qualey can fly you out to safety that night."

"Then you're letting Phil Qualey go back with me."

He nodded. "He'll need the time, to fix that broken pontoon." He looked at her and tried a faint smile. "I think you can handle him. Just make sure he doesn't fly off without giving us the time to get back. Or without *you*."

She grinned. "What do you expect me to do if he tries, shoot him?"

Instantly she knew she'd said the wrong thing. His smile vanished.

"You mean," he said bitterly, "like I'd do."

"No, that isn't what I meant at all. It was supposed to be a joke. You're too sensitive, Captain."

Shaw went on tightly as though she hadn't spoken: "All you have to do is *threaten* to shoot him and sound like you mean it. That should be enough to keep him in line."

He stared off at the jungle below again, his face hard. "I guess you think I'm some kind of unfeeling monster, the way I've taken on the responsibility for possibly killing those nineteen prisoners down there."

She thought about it before answering. "No. I just think you're a man with the strength to do whatever *has* to be done. If those prisoners do die, it'll be necessity that killed them, not you."

He shook his head, still gazing away. "That's a pretty way to put it. But I'm still the conscious instrument of that necessity."

"I know . . . and I know if it happens *you'll* feel their

deaths more than anyone else. I don't think you'll be able to live with it afterwards."

He looked at her then, his eyes almost desperate. "I'm already living with worse. I can take that much more, if I have to."

She shook her head. "That's your trouble," she told him softly, "trying to make it all by yourself, carrying the past around inside you like a broken bottle of acid. You're going to come apart soon, Captain. Unless you've got someone who cares for you, to help you."

He stared at her, startled again by her openness.

She raised and lowered her shoulders in a slow shrug. "I learned long ago, if you don't reach out for what you need and want, it'll pass you by. And you never get the chance again."

Qualey finished eating and got a small, battered pewter flask from his pocket. He unscrewed the cap, took a long swallow of gin, and then handed it over to Flood.

He watched as Flood tilted the flask to his mouth. "Go easy on it. That's all I've got."

Flood swallowed and handed it back. Qualey started to screw the cap on, then hesitated, looking toward Corporal Miller. He got up and walked over to Miller, as Flood stood up and stretched himself lazily.

Qualey held out the flask dubiously. "Hey kid, you *sure* you don't drink?"

Miller grinned up at him. "Don't take it so hard, old timer. I'm not a complete teetotaler. Now if that was a nice cool half of ale . . ."

"Sure, and if I was Charlie Lindbergh . . ." Qualey shrugged, screwing the cap back on the flask as he started to turn away.

He froze half-turned, staring in terror. "Oh my *God!* . . ."

Corporal Miller snatched up his submachine gun and came up off the ground twisting toward the direction in which Qualey was staring. All in one smooth, incredibly swift movement.

Flood went past behind him with two long strides, grabbed one of the explosives bundles, and threw it over the cliff.

He was bending for the second one when Corporal Miller twisted back and clubbed him across the back of the head with his forearm. Again his speed of reaction was incredible. But it wasn't fast enough. Flood shoved the remaining explosives over the edge as he sprawled to the ground.

Desperately, Miller threw himself flat beside Flood, reaching over the edge for it. One fingertip touched the canvas as the bundle fell away from him. He lay there and watched in horror as it followed the first, which had already vanished; smashing apart in the rapids far below, and being swept out of sight over one of the series of waterfalls.

Flood shoved up on one elbow and put a hand to his aching head and badly wrenched neck. But he forgot about the pain when he saw Captain Shaw standing over him, staring down at him.

There was madness in Shaw's eyes. As though unaware consciously of what he was doing, Shaw reached down a hand and slowly drew the service revolver from its belt holster. He cocked it, aiming down at Flood's face as his finger slid across the trigger.

"Don't!" Nora screamed.

"Don't. . . ." Flood repeated the word, but managed to keep it from being a scream. He went on quickly but distinctly, knowing he had to make every word get through to the enraged man standing over him: "You'll *need* me now. I know how you can do the job without those mines. But you're going to need every one of us—to get it done the only way left. My way."

There was a long moment in which Shaw remained frozen in killing position, aiming the gun down at Flood's face, finger ready to twitch against the trigger. Then, slowly, the insanity ebbed from his eyes. He let the fist holding the gun fall to his side.

"What*ever* happens," he whispered through his teeth, "if we're still alive when it's over, I'm going to make sure you get what's coming to you for this. That I swear to you."

Flood drew a shaky breath, knowing how close he'd been. If he'd known the officer was crazy, he'd never had tried it that way.

"I'll worry about that when the time comes," he said mildly, sitting up on the ground and rubbing the ache where Miller had hit him. "Now, you ready to hear *my* plan?"

Qualey was staring at him, registering his treachery. "You dirty bastard . . . you were just using me . . . playing me for a fool. . . ." But there was a reluctant undertone of grudging admiration in his words.

Flood nodded without looking at him, keeping his attention on Shaw, whose lean cheeks were still mottled with red spots of fury. Quickly he outlined his own idea on how to destroy the enemy base.

Shaw heard him out in silence, with no change in expression. "You know as well as I do how little chance this has of succeeding," he rasped finally.

"More chance than those prisoners would have had, doing it your way. Of course, if you can think of something better? . . ."

Shaw shook his head. "There's no other way left to us. Not now. You knew that."

He hunkered down on the ground facing Flood. With the mutual hatred still livid between them, they carefully went over the details of the new plan; modifying it, refining it, timing it.

By the time they were finished, Qualey knew the full extent of Flood's treachery toward him. Furiously, he objected to the part he was expected to play in the operation now: "The *Skylark* ain't a warplane! And I'm a civilian! You got no right at all, under any kind of law, to make me risk me and my plane like that. I won't do it."

Shaw turned his head and looked at Qualey without expression for a moment. He was very aware of Nora's presence at that moment, though he didn't look at her. When he spoke, his voice was surprisingly gentle.

"Qualey, that old plane of yours has just about seen its

last days anyhow. What are you going to do after it quits flying? I know you don't have the money to buy another. How do you expect to go on making a living?"

Qualey scowled at him, unable to contradict him. "There's still *me*. I got my life to think of."

Shaw nodded. "And your future. All right. After this is over, I'll buy you a new plane. Or a secondhand plane that's a bit bigger and still in good condition. Your choice. You have my word on it."

Qualey was suddenly confused. "You got that kind of money? I didn't know you were rich."

"I'm not rich. But I have enough for what I'm promising you." There was a barely perceptible break in his voice. "I don't have anyone else to spend it on."

Qualey mulled it over, tasting the temptation. It would put him back in business. Solidly. Greed and fear struggled inside his guts.

"A *two*-engine job? Room for six passengers?"

Shaw nodded. "I think I could manage that."

"You're giving me your word, in front of witnesses. That's like a legal contract."

"I understand. I intend to honor it."

"Sure . . . if you can." Qualey studied Shaw shrewdly. "Tell me something, Captain. Do I really have any choice? I mean, you're holding up a carrot in front of me, but you're still ready with that stick. Right? What happens if I say no?"

"I'll shoot you. And try to fly your plane myself."

"That's what I figured," Qualey said dryly. He looked a bit relieved to have the decision taken off his hands. "In that case . . . I guess it's a deal."

Shaw turned back to Flood. "That leaves us with the problem of finding the grenades and pistols we'll need."

"We could surprise one of those patrols the base sends out on either side of the river. . . ."

Shaw shook his head. "No. That would alert the base to trouble. And destroy any hope we have of getting inside there undetected." He mulled it over and came to a hard decision: "We'll have to double back and try to catch the patrol that passed us this morning."

Flood scowled at him. "They were headed up into the mountains. By now they could be all the way to . . ."

"I don't think so," Shaw cut in. "They weren't carrying enough equipment and provisions to set up a night camp. Looked to me like a half-day patrol. Coming from their base when we saw them; so by now they'll be heading home—in this general direction."

It was Miller who was frowning at him now. "But sir, even if you're right . . . won't we be using up a lot of valuable time?"

Shaw nodded grimly, still looking at Flood. "We'll just have to make up that time, somehow. There's no other way now."

They started out minutes later, turning back the way they'd come, to try taking by force what they would need to carry out the operation the new way. As they moved quickly up through the mountains, Shaw dropped back beside Flood.

"I meant what I said earlier," he told Flood tightly. "If this mission fails, it'll be because you sabotaged our chances. You'll spend the rest of your life in prison for that."

Flood shrugged carelessly. "No I won't. If it fails we'll all be dead and past doing anything. If it just happens to work, no one'll care how we did it. They'll forget about me and give you a medal—though they might still have to pin it on your grave."

NINE

The eleven-man patrol came down the mountain slope moving briskly in spite of the leg-weariness from half a day of climbing. They were eager to get back to their base camp, get their boots off, and have a hot meal. In their swing through the upper slopes they'd found nothing to alert them to trouble, which was as they'd expected. New Britain was securely in Japanese hands. But they didn't neglect elementary precautions. As they entered the narrow, deeply shadowed trail which twisted through the jungle, one trooper was sent on well ahead, acting as a scout.

With his patrol out of sight behind him, the scout slowed his pace a bit. He followed the sharp twists in the narrow trail, trudging heavily on feet that felt painfully swollen in boots that were too tight for him. Coming to a small stream, he paused and looked across. The jungle was a solid wall on the other side. He couldn't see into it.

Angling toward where the trail continued on the other side, he waded across. The water was shallow, coming up only to his ankles. He came out of the stream enjoying the soothing sensation of the cold water that had seeped through his boots.

There was no warning of another presence as he started into the continuation of the trail. Suddenly Shaw was behind him, one hand clamping across his nose and mouth, the other arm wrapping around him chest-high, pinning his arms and rifle to his body. The scout struggled uselessly and tried to get his mouth open far enough to bite at the hand stifling his outcry.

He never got the chance. Corporal Miller loomed in front of him, driving the long, two-edged blade of his commando knife into him just below the breast bone.

Holding the feebly jerking scout between them, Shaw and Miller faded back into the jungle with him. When they were hidden behind a tangle of vines and bushes, they stopped, but continued to hold the scout tightly between them until his legs stopped quivering and hung loosely.

Miller twisted the knife free and stooped to clean the blade by plunging it into the dirt. Shaw carefully lowered the dead man to the ground. Unslinging his tommy gun, he worked his way through the jungle edging the stream until he came to where Flood and Qualey were waiting. They were crouched behind the bushes, each holding a rifle ready. Nora was out of sight in the protection of a boulder a short distance behind them, holding the .45 automatic in both hands, just in case. The foldboat was with her.

Shaw hunkered down to Qualey's right. Miller moved around behind them and took up his position on Flood's left. Shaw's orders had been specific. He and Miller would commence firing at either flank of the patrol and work inward. Flood and Qualey were to concentrate their rifle fire on the middle men and work outward.

That was if the enemy patrol fanned out. If they did not, it was going to be harder. Much harder. Shaw and Miller would strike at the men in the rear and try to cut off any retreat, while Flood and Qualey cut down the men in front. Either way, the important thing was that none of the enemy must be allowed to get away and bring his whole garrison back after them.

The four of them waited silently for the other ten men of the patrol to appear. Shaw turned his head and glanced at Qualey. The aging pilot was holding his rifle tightly and taking short careful breaths through his open mouth. He looked nervous, but not quite as frightened as Shaw had expected. On the other side of Qualey, Flood waited wooden-faced, his eyes narrowed to slits. The only expression on the face of Miller was one of frowning concentration on the moments ahead.

Shaw thought about Nora hidden behind them. Then he cleared his mind of her and peered through the vines and big hanging leaves at the stream. He remembered the fear and kill-lust that had run through him while watching the patrol go past that morning. Neither was with him now. He felt only cool, single-minded preoccupation with a job that needed to be done quickly and efficiently.

The first enemy troopers came out of the jungle on the other side of the stream. Shaw slid his finger across the trigger of his submachine gun as the rest emerged, praying for them to spread out the way a patrol was supposed to when fording a stream.

But they didn't. The first five started across the stream bunched together. The other five straggled into the water behind them.

Suppressing a groan of disappointment, Shaw sighted along the short barrel at the rear man on the right. He waited until the trooper entered the stream on the other side. He would have preferred to wait until his target was halfway across, but the lead members of the enemy patrol were already coming out of the water on the near bank. Another couple steps and they'd be too close.

Aiming at the rear trooper's knees to compensate for the anticipated upward buck of the submachine gun, Shaw gave the trigger a brief squeeze. The explosive stammer of the short burst hurt his eardrums, the muzzle jerking up in spite of his efforts to hold it down. Three steel-jacketed slugs shot across the stream. The first hit the water, the second went low into the enemy soldier's stomach, and the third smashed his chest, twisting and dropping him.

Even before the man sprawled dead on the opposite bank with his legs in the water, the three men to Shaw's left were firing. The staccato roars of the machine guns and the sharp blasts of the rifles punctuated the screaming of men caught and dying in the point-blank barrage.

Qualey's and Flood's rifles dropped the two nearest troopers back into the water. A long, low burst from Miller's tommy gun ripped two more of the rearmost enemy apart, as the survivors scrambled desperately to get back across the stream to the protection of the jungle. One was almost into the bushes there when a burst from Shaw stitched high across his back, pinning him momentarily to the trunk of a tree before he sank down in an inert heap against its base.

One of the soldiers who had been in the lead had yanked a grenade from his belt and pulled the pin as he charged away across the stream. He paused near the opposite bank, twisting to throw it at the ambushers. Bullets fired by Flood and Qualey ripped his midsection open. He sank down with the grenade still in his opening fingers. The explosion lifted his body clear out of the water again. It also dropped another enemy soldier at the edge of the jungle.

An enemy who had been downed by Miller's first burst was on his hands and knees, crawling into the brush. Another burst from Miller and two snap shots from Flood caught him and flopped him over on his back like a broken puppet. That left three of the patrol still on their feet, racing to the wall of jungle on the other side of the stream. The weapons of all four ambushers swung after them in a raggedly crashing volley.

The last of the three jerked, spun, and toppled face-forward back into the water. But the first plunged on into the jungle. The second seemed to trip, then recovered and lunged forward in a low crouch, vanishing from sight after the first one.

In the sudden silence, Flood rose from his knee cursing softly.

Qualey nodded unhappily. *"Two* we missed. . . ."

But Shaw was already on his feet, moving out with his submachine gun. "Guard Mrs. Ferguson and that boat!" he snarled at Flood and Qualey; and then he was sprinting across the stream, followed by Miller.

They went into the jungle on the other side at different angles, but acting in concert as a well-drilled team.

Miller pushed swiftly through the thick foliage siding the trail on the other side, looking for some sign of the direction the escaping enemy pair had taken. Unable to find any, he stopped and listened intently. There was nothing to hear. Sweating profusely in the stifling wet heat, Miller moved to the very edge of the trail and listened again. Still he could hear nothing, not even Shaw, though he knew the Captain must be very close.

Drawing a deep breath, Miller darted straight across the trail, deliberately showing himself to draw fire. He was in the open only a split second, the small of his back knotting in a spasm of fear. Then he was into the dense vegetation on the other side. Nothing had happened.

He turned toward the trail again. Bending slightly at the knees, he stepped out into the trail for one terrifying instant. Then he dove headfirst into the bushes on the other side.

A rifle crashed loudly somewhere behind him. Something whispered through the air above his moving figure, through the space where his torso had been before he dived. He hit the ground behind the bushes on one shoulder and did a fast roll. Having no accurate idea where the shot had come from, he next lay very still, waiting.

On the other side of the trail the enemy sniper sat behind a clump of brush, working the bolt action of his rifle. His right leg was stretched out, bleeding where the bullet had gone in as he scrambled from the stream. Taking aim across the trail at the place where Miller had vanished, he fired into the bushes blindly. He was quickly working another cartridge into the chamber when he heard a faint sound behind him.

He tried to twist around from the sitting position, and

started to cry out a warning. The cry was cut short as the stock of Shaw's tommy gun crushed in the side of his skull. But it was sufficient to alert the other hidden sniper. Shaw whipped around bringing the gun up in firing position.

The rifle shot came from where he least expected it: the lower branches of a huge tree. The bullet slashed his side, twisting him off his feet. He hit the ground with a gasp of agony. Quickly, he rolled for the only protection near enough, a fallen tree.

He managed to get behind it, but once there he was pinned down. He couldn't even raise his head to look over the tree trunk. With the downward angle the remaining sniper had on him, he'd get the top of his skull blown off. Shaw could only lie where he was, listening, and feeling his blood leak from the burning wound in his side.

It took only a second for the sniper also to realize that Shaw was pinned in position. Lowering himself silently from his tree branch, he began circling sideways, holding the rifle ready for the killing shot.

Four utterly silent steps, and he could see Shaw behind the fallen tree, his face down in the dirt. He took aim at Shaw's back.

A concentrated machine gun burst got him waist-high, almost tearing him in half.

Corporal Miller stepped from the bushes, lowering his tommy gun as he moved around the man he'd killed. His eyes widened as Shaw got to his feet, and he saw the sticky redness staining the whole side of his shirt.

"Sir, you're hit. . . ."

Shaw nodded and started back toward the stream. Miller moved to help him, but Shaw shook his head. "It's not that bad."

When they reached the stream, Miller called out to the others. Flood, Qualey, and Nora emerged as they got to the other side. Nora saw Shaw's blood-soaked shirt. She didn't gasp or grimace. Her mouth just tightened slightly, and she hurried toward him.

But Shaw suddenly turned away from her, staring at the opposite bank of the stream.

The others caught the shock on his face and looked in

the same direction—at the place where the second enemy soldier had fallen when the grenade exploded.

The "body" was no longer there.

Miller was the first to react: "Must have only been hurt. Crawled off when . . ."

"Unless he was just playing dead all the time," Qualey cut in.

Shaw nodded and looked at Corporal Miller.

"I'll try, sir." Miller instantly started back across the stream to search for the missing enemy.

Flood grabbed the tommy gun from Shaw's hand and went after him. Shaw started to object, but changed his mind.

"Fifteen minutes," he flung after them through pain-clenched teeth. "That's all you've got. We've already used up too much time on this."

Then he began helping Nora, who was single-mindedly unbuttoning his shirt. When they got it off, she looked critically at the wound.

"You're lucky the bullet's not in you. But it's not good."

"I'll be all right if we can stop the bleeding." Shaw sat down on the stream bank and began washing out the wound with the cold water. "Tear the shirt into strips for bandaging."

Qualey was already moving from one dead trooper to another, gathering up what they had ambushed the patrol to get: grenades and handguns. By the time he had all of them, Nora was finishing tying the strips of cloth around Shaw to hold the thicker pad of material tightly to his cleaned wound. It was still bleeding, but not as profusely.

The number of grenades Qualey had found was more than they'd hoped for: twenty-two of them. But the handguns were a disappointment. There had been only two 8mm. Nambu automatics among the entire patrol.

"They'll have to do," Shaw said after a moment.

Qualey frowned at him. "But that only makes five handguns, together with the .45 and yours and the corporal's."

"They'll have to do," Shaw repeated flatly.

Miller and Flood came back from their search. They didn't have to speak. A look at their faces showed that they hadn't found the missing enemy soldier.

"He could be holed-up close by," Miller said dubiously, "but I couldn't spot him."

"It's more likely he's halfway back to his home base by now," Shaw said. He rose to his feet. "We've got to get away from here, fast. And leave as little trail as possible for them to follow."

Quickly, he supervised the division of the spoils. All the grenades to Qualey and Nora; except six, two each for Shaw, Miller, and Flood. Shaw stuck one of the Nambu automatics in his belt, and Flood did the same with the other one and the Colt .45. Miller kept his submachine gun, and Flood held on to Shaw's. The less Shaw had to carry, the quicker the bullet rip in his side would stop bleeding.

Shaw turned to Qualey and Nora. "It's best if we split up now. I can find my way back to the river without any trouble. And you're going to need all the time we've got left to repair the plane."

"That's for sure," Qualey agreed thinly.

"Remember," Shaw told him pointedly, "you've got to hit tomorrow an hour before dusk. Exactly."

That was the crux of the whole operation now. The assault on the base had to come during the day, while the torpedo boats were still there. But close enough to dark so the enemy would have little chance of sealing up the straits by some other method—for one single night at least.

He checked his watch against Qualey's, pinpointing the time of the two-pronged assault.

"I'll do my best," Qualey said. "No way the *Skylark* can take off until we fix that float. . . ."

"Be there," Shaw snapped. "On time."

"We'll be there," Nora assured him. Her tone was quiet, but there was no trace of uncertainty in it.

Shaw looked at her alone then. After a moment he put his hands on her shoulders, the gesture surprising himself more than her. "I'm sorry for the part you have to play in this. If there was any other way . . ."

She reached up and took his face between her hands, pulled his mouth down to hers and kissed him lightly.

"Be careful. . . ." she whispered. "Take care of yourself. . . ."

The others stared at the two of them, startled. Qualey grinned crookedly. "Well, what d'you know. . . ."

Nora stepped back from Shaw, still looking at him. "Captain . . . do you *have* a first name?"

"Michael," Shaw told her. "Mike."

She nodded to herself, went on studying him a moment. Then she picked up her half of the grenades, turned, and began the hike back up toward the coastwatcher shack. Qualey went after her, lugging the rest of the grenades.

Shaw watched them go, then led Miller and Flood into the brush. Getting the inflatable foldboat, they headed toward the river with it.

It was two hours later that thirty heavily armed Japanese soldiers from the base reached the spot where the patrol had been ambushed. The lieutenant in command studied the bodies sprawled in and around the stream and sent some of his men to circle the area for signs of the ambushers' trail.

He looked up at sounds in the sky above him. And saw two observation planes, sent from the nearest airfield. They circled overhead twice and then separated. One flew off over the upper slopes of the mountains. The other went hunting above the lower reaches of the jungle.

The scouts returned without finding any evidence of the direction the unknown enemy had taken. The lieutenant followed the example of the observation planes. He divided his big search party in two parts. Half his men he led up the mountain slope in the direction Nora and Qualey had taken. The other half, led by a sergeant, headed down through the jungle.

Nora and Qualey were lucky. When the observation plane appeared overhead, they were climbing a forested slope, hidden by the trees. They stopped and squinted upward through the overhanging branches, knowing they could not be seen in turn. The plane kept flying in slow figure eights that got farther and farther away. When it was gone, they resumed their climbing. . . .

Captain Shaw's group was not that lucky. When the observation plane appeared they were on the ledge above the river, a short distance below where Flood had kicked the explosives over the cliff. They had stopped in the open, in plain sight, to transfer the carrying of the foldboat from Miller to Flood for a time. And they didn't hear the plane until it suddenly flew directly above them.

Scrambling into the shadows of some boulders, they watched the plane fly on for several seconds, and dared to hope. Then the plane was turning, circling lower as it came back towards them. It was obvious they'd been spotted.

"Come *on*," Shaw grated. He began running down the ledge, toward the fringe of the jungle below.

He was slowed by his wound and loss of blood. Corporal Miller sprinted past him easily. Flood, even burdened by the foldboat, managed to keep up with Shaw.

The plane roared past directly over their heads, and disappeared for a time. It reappeared, circling back, as they dodged into the jungle where it could no longer see them. The three men stopped, panting, peering up through the thick foliage.

The plane began flying low, lazy circles over the spot where they'd vanished into the jungle. What looked like an aluminum can fell from it.

The can hit the ground a hundred yards from the hiding men and exploded, spewing out a dazzling white magnesium glare.

The three men blinked, momentarily blinded by the brilliance of the explosion.

Miller opened his eyes cautiously. "Incendiaries! Fixing our location for a search party . . ."

A dark cloud began rising from the point where the can had hit. It became a black pillar reaching toward the sky as a second incendiary can toppled from the circling plane.

"Move!" Shaw snarled. "Just keep going! They can't see where we're going as long as we stick to the brush!"

The three of them began to run again.

It was true that the circling observation plane could not see them through the overhang of the jungle. So it was only blind, terrible chance that directed the fall of the third cannister.

Corporal Miller was running well ahead of Shaw and Flood. The can hit a tree trunk directly in front of him. The explosion showered instantly igniting magnesium all over both the tree and Miller. The next instant both were utterly engulfed in hissing, glaring flame.

Shaw and Flood froze, staring in unbelieving horror at a section of flame, the magnesium still igniting, thrashing about on the ground. They could not see Miller inside that sputtering white segment of flame. But they could hear the howling that came from within it, a sound that had nothing human about it.

Flood fell to his knees and threw up. Shaw remained standing; rigid, staring. The howling ended. When Flood looked up, the flame-hidden figure on the ground was no longer moving. The blazing chemical fire that had once been Miller continued to burn, its smoke rising to join the smoke from the burning tree and surrounding vegetation. In the sky above, the observation plane was flying away.

Flood shoved to his feet, grabbed Shaw's arm and tugged.

"Come *on!*"

He had to pull again before Shaw moved, turning away from the fire that had once been Miller. He yanked his arm from Flood's grasp and began hiking down the slope, moving with long, steady strides as they resumed their trek toward the river.

For a long time the two men kept going in silence. Shaw didn't look at Flood, not once. Not even when, after over an hour, he finally spoke to him.

"One more small item for that delicate conscience of yours," Shaw said without any expression in his voice at all. "You killed him. Destroying the explosives. You know that."

Flood kept on, silent. There was nothing he could say to that. Shaw was undoubtedly right.

For a time Shaw did not speak again. Then he said, in that same flat, toneless voice: "I'm not going to send you to prison, after all. *Whatever* else happens, Flood—if we're both alive at the end—I'm going to shoot you dead. Personally. You have my word on that."

Flood said nothing to that, either. But he knew absolutely that Shaw meant what he'd just said and would go on meaning it. He didn't know why young Corporal Miller had meant so much to Shaw. He didn't know about Shaw's dead son whom Miller had resembled.

But he did know this: he and Shaw wouldn't both come out of this alive. One of them was going to have to die.

The lieutenant in command of the search party combing the upper slopes of the mountains saw the columns of smoke far below. He understood what it meant, and for a few moments he debated heading back down. But then he decided that what was going on below was the concern of the other half of the search party down there. His concern was making sure there were no more of the enemy in the area above.

He continued upward until it became too dark to see the way. Then he called in his flanked-out men and instructed them to make camp for the night. The place where they settled down was less than four miles from the Ferguson coastwatcher shack. And the crippled *Skylark*.

TEN

It was dark long before they reached the river. They were into the level lowlands by then, and without downward sloping ground to guide them, they had to make it the rest of the way on little more than instinct and a continual bearing toward their left. There was a space of time, almost an hour, during which they worked their way blindly through the dark undergrowth, increasingly afraid they'd become lost—until finally they heard the river ahead of them.

They could hear, but not see it. The closer they got to the river, the thicker the jungle became. For the last hundred yards or so Flood had to hack their way through with Shaw's commando knife. Guided by the shine of Shaw's flashlight he slashed and chopped, panting and sweating, gulping his lungs full of muggy, rot-smelling air.

At last they got through, and sank down wearily on the bank of the smooth, swift-running river. Flood gratefully eased the foldboat from his shoulders. Shaw put the flashlight on the ground, still switched on, and got a small bottle from his pocket. In the yellow glow of the flashlight, Flood could see what the wound, loss of blood, and the hard trek had done to Shaw. His face had become gaunt, the cheeks sunken, the eyes feverish. He seemed to have difficulty with his left arm, the side with the wound. Blood had run down his side from under the improvised bandaging.

Shaking two pills from the bottle onto his palm, Shaw popped them in his mouth and washed them down with a swallow of water from his canteen. He tilted two more pills into his palm, held them out to Flood.

Flood took them uncertainly. "What's this?"

"Stimulant." Shaw's voice was thin with fatigue. "Something to keep us going. We'll need it."

Flood nodded and swallowed the pills with a gulp of water. They *were* going to need it. There'd be little sleep for them that night or all through the next day. There was too much to be done, especially before dawn; and they were behind schedule. With Shaw's plan, a possible rescue of the prisoners in the base had been incidental to the operation. But Flood's way, the whole operation depended on freeing the prisoners; it couldn't be done without their help. And that was going to take some doing.

Shaw quickly tallied the weapons they had to do it with. Four handguns: the Colt .45 and the Nambu automatic in Flood's belt, the Nambu in Shaw's belt, and the Enfield .38 in his holster. One Thompson submachine gun. A commando knife. Four hand grenades. That was all. It would have to do.

Shaw began undoing the canvas wrapped around the inflatable foldboat. If he was still dwelling on Miller's sickening death, it was now firmly sealed off in the back of his brain; the rest of him was concentrated on the job again.

Flood helped him with the canvas, pulling it away from the two short paddles and heavy folds of rubber. Now that they had reached this place, he was anxious to get away from it. There was something evil and oppressive about the tropic night here. The massive lushness of the looming walls of vegetation felt somehow overwhelming; as though about to close in, smothering and crushing them. A steamy mist rose off the dark surface of the river. With the jungle keeping out any trace of breeze, the haze hung there in the hot, fetid air, making it difficult to breathe.

It was not a place for a person with claustrophobia. They were surrounded and overhung with explosive growth and malignant decay. Ferns grew as big as trees. The trees were hung and interlaced and strangled in networks of vines. There were enormous masses of repulsive parasitic growths in the shapes of gigantic sponges, distorted mushrooms, balloons, and hanging curtains; soft and ugly.

And soon, adding to the eagerness to get out on the river and on their way, came the mosquitoes and stinging flies, attacking them in whining clouds. Flood and Shaw had come partly prepared for this. They had mosquito netting from the coastwatcher shack to hang from their bush hats, protecting their faces and necks. But Shaw's torso was almost entirely bare, and the swarming insects were attracted by the blood from his wounded side.

Shaw snatched the knife from Flood and slashed a hole in the canvas that had been wrapped around the foldboat. Pushing his head and neck through the hole, he draped the canvas around him like a poncho, covering his torso and arms. But clouds of flying insects kept attacking, concentrating now on their hands.

With fingers rapidly swelling from the insect bites, the two men worked quickly to get the boat inflated. There were two cylindrical cartridges attached to the heavy folds of rubber. Shaw tugged the ring in one cartridge; Flood pulled at the other. There were two sharp popping sounds from the cartridges, followed by a loud hissing as air rushed out of them. The heavy rubber began unfolding as it filled with the air, swelling rapidly. Within seconds the ungainly mass of rubber had become a sturdy boat with balloon sides.

Shaw and Flood pushed it into the water and climbed in with the paddles. The strong current caught at the rubber boat, swirled it out into midriver, and began carrying them swiftly toward their destination. The boat had been fashioned to carry three men as a normal load; four in a pinch.

For two, there was plenty of leg room. For a while, at least, it was going to be a comfortable, restful journey downriver. With the current doing the work for them, all that was required was an occasional touch of the paddle to keep the boat from snagging on the banks or a rare midstream obstruction.

"You could grab an hour's sleep now," Flood suggested to Shaw. "You look like you need it."

Shaw's night-shadowed face looked at him for a moment. Then he pulled in his paddle and curled up on his right side, favoring his wound. Exhaustion brought sleep to him almost immediately.

Flood dipped his paddle into the water to get the boat angled back in the middle of the river. He leaned against the balloon side, stretching out his legs, and savored being off them at last. The stimulant pills were already taking effect. The tiredness was seeping out of his body. He felt wide-awake, his brain clear and alert.

The movement of air as the boat was swept down the river was refreshing. The mosquitoes and flies no longer came in clouds, but only as occasional, minor annoyances. Flood dipped in his paddle from time to time, the faint splashes joining the other sounds of the tropic night: the gurgling of the river against the banks, the noises of snakes and small animals in the underbrush on either side, the shrieks of night birds.

More than an hour passed, and the nature of the river began to change. The current was no longer as swift, and Flood had to start digging in with his paddle to keep the rubber boat in steady motion. But still he didn't wake Shaw. He wanted Shaw to get as much rest as possible. And he didn't want him opening up that wound again with too much hard paddling.

There was nothing altruistic about this. Flood knew his own capabilities and also what he lacked. Shaw had been *trained* to do the kind of job they were headed for. Pulling it off was going to depend on him more than Flood. Flood wanted him to be able to act fast and think fast when the time came.

He glanced at Shaw curled on his side asleep—and

found himself remembering Corporal Miller. Savagely, he wiped the memory of Miller from his mind. He was sure he had done the right thing when he'd kicked those limpet mines and time fuses off the cliff. Right or wrong, he'd done it—and for a reason. He tore his gaze away from Shaw and looked ahead, his face settling into a stubborn, sullen expression. He paddled with long, hard strokes, driving the boat toward the enemy base hidden where the river reached the sea.

The water was becoming muddy. In places the right bank was not earth at all, but tangled networks of tree roots twisting up out of the water. When he came to a place where the river divided, he was expecting it. They had studied the course of the river on Shaw's detail map. The right fork dispersed into a swamp. Flood turned the boat into the left fork.

This branch of the river was narrower, the jungle almost shutting out the stars overhead. As Flood paddled through it, the jungle became interspersed with marshes that gave off an unpleasant odor similar to decaying garbage. The water became brackish, the current slowing to a drift.

Flood suddenly leaned forward, squinting, seeing something in the darkness ahead. As the boat drifted closer, he saw what it was: another branching of the river. He prodded the sleeping Shaw with the toe of his boot.

Shaw woke and sat up straight immediately, looking around him. "We're at the fork. . . ."

"The second one. That means we're getting close."

Shaw peered at the luminous dial of his waterproof watch, then looked up sharply at Flood. "You were supposed to wake me."

"I just did," Flood said flatly. "Time to start being careful. Both of us. Keep our eyes and ears open."

Shaw started to say something, then just nodded and picked up the other paddle.

"*I'll* do the paddling," Flood told him. "You concentrate on keeping a sharp lookout. We don't know if they've got patrols out at night. Or how far up this river they come."

Shaw considered it. His left arm felt in working order, though a bit stiff. But the improvised bandaging under his canvas poncho was caked dry now, and he didn't want the wound to open up again with so much time still to go.

"You've been doing all the paddling alone so far," he pointed out. "You won't be any good to me if you wear yourself out."

"When I'm tired I'll tell you. So far, those pills are doing a great job."

Shaw hesitated a moment longer, then turned forward, peering into the darkness ahead, listening intently to the night sounds as Flood paddled the boat into the right fork of the river.

Flood used the paddle with more care now, trying to make as little noise as possible. They were in the final branch of the river, the one that led directly to the enemy base. The closer they got, the greater the danger. Exactly what that danger was in this stretch of the river, they didn't know. Only one thing was certain, it was growing with each passing second.

They had been moving through this final branch of the river for about half an hour when the boat was suddenly stopped by an unseen barrier. Shaw was leaning forward, and the jarring halt threw him farther forward. His mouth struck a taut wire that bit his upper lip back into his teeth. He jerked his head back, tasting blood in his mouth.

"What the hell is it?" Flood whispered. The rubber boat was stopped dead in the water, and he couldn't make out what was doing it.

Shaw fumbled around and found the flashlight. He snapped it on, shielding the glass with one hand so only a little light escaped. It glinted on three strands of thick fencing wire strung tightly across the width of the river, the ends fastened to tree trunks on the banks. The lowest strand was just inches above the water, and this was the one stopping the rubber boat. The middle strand was on a level with their faces. The highest one was several feet above their heads.

"*One* of the things I didn't know about," Flood commented dryly. "Easy enough to cut through, though. *If* we wanted."

Shaw shook his head. "We don't. Now we know how far those patrols come. A break in the wire would tell them we're inside. Or someone is. We'll have to portage around this."

It was as though his words were a prophecy about to be fulfilled. He had barely snapped off the light when they both heard it: the chugging of a small engine coming up the river in their direction.

A split-second later they saw the flash of a searchlight switching through the jungle foliage.

Shaw pointed to the right bank and snatched up the other paddle. They dug the paddles deep in the water with long, hard strokes; but very careful not to make any splashing noises. The rubber boat swung toward the bank. The sound of the chugging engine came swiftly closer. They dug the paddles in harder, driving the rubber boat through the water.

It reached the bank, nosed into the soft mud there. Behind them the beam of the searchlight swung through the jungle foliage, reaching for them. Only one short bend in the river separated them from it now. The chugging was very loud, very near.

Shaw and Flood jumped out into the mud, pulled the rubber boat after them up onto the soft bank of the river. They kept pulling it as they pushed themselves in through the dense ferns growing at the water's edge. When they had all of the boat hidden within the ferns they dropped flat, squinting out at the dark river, clenching their teeth to still their breathing.

A small open motorboat came around the bend. There was one enemy trooper in the stern working the outboard motor and tiller. Another in the bow operated the powerful searchlight, swinging it from side to side. Between them sat four troopers armed with semiautomatic rifles tipped by bayonets.

A river patrol from the base. Another thing Flood hadn't known about.

The motorboat slowed to a drift as it reached the wire barrier. The trooper in the bow shined the searchlight on the three strands of wire, then swung it at one of the banks of the river on the other side of the wires—the bank where the two men with the rubber boat were hidden.

Flood and Shaw ducked their heads as the beam of the searchlight laced back and forth past their hiding place, getting lower each time. The last time, it shined directly at them for a long moment. But apparently the reflected glare off the ferns concealed them effectively. The searchlight swung away to the opposite bank of the river.

The two hidden men did not move. They watched as the searchlight illuminated the jungle across the river from them, and then probed the darkness upriver.

At last, the inspection was over. The motorboat backed and turned. It began chugging away downriver, its searchlight swinging back and forth from bank to bank.

Flood and Shaw waited silently until they could no longer see any gleam of the searchlight; continued to wait until they could no longer hear the chugging engine. Then they rose to their feet, looking at the blur of each other's face in the jungle dark. Stinging insects were at them again, but they slapped at them mechanically, hardly noticing.

"So much for the portage idea," Shaw said finally.

Flood nodded. "Can't go on the river any further. No telling how often that boat comes back."

"Exactly. We'll have to walk it from here."

Flood looked down regretfully at the rubber boat. "We better sink it in the river. Less chance of them finding it."

"Yes."

Shaw stooped and got the flashlight from the boat, stuck it in his belt. Flood got the submachine gun and slung it on his shoulder. Everything else they'd need they were already carrying. Shaw drew his knife and stabbed it into the boat's balloon side. There was a great whooshing of air escaping through the rip as the boat deflated. In seconds it was nothing but heavy folds of rubber once more.

Flood watched, puzzled for a moment, as Shaw continued to slash at the rubber, cutting carefully at what had been the bottom of the boat. "Waterproof bags? . . ."

"That's right." Shaw continued to cut until he had two large rough squares of rubber sliced free. He rose, giving one to Flood. They stuck them in their belts, ready for when they'd need them. Then they began hunting around for rocks and stones.

Ten minutes later, the remains of the rubber boat were in the mud at the bottom of the river, wrapped around the two paddles and weighted down with stones they'd managed to find. As soon as it was done they set out, angling into the jungle but never straying far from the river that would lead them to their goal.

Shaw led the way. Flood followed him closely, making no suggestions, depending utterly on Shaw's commando training to keep them out of the hands of base patrols and night lookouts.

IV

The
Assault

ELEVEN

They were close enough to hear the river, off to their left. Shaw moved in a parallel course to it, crawling through the jungle undergrowth on his hands and knees. For the past half hour he had not risen from his knees, and he was avoiding any trail they came across. Every twenty seconds he stopped and listened for a time before moving on.

Flood crawled behind him, his hands and knees sinking into the spongy ground. He couldn't move the way Shaw did, totally silent; but he worked his way through as quietly as he could. Ahead of him, Shaw suddenly stopped. Flood immediately did the same, squinting past him into the murky blackness. It took him a moment to see they'd reached the edge of a small natural clearing.

Shaw listened for a few seconds. Hearing nothing, he began crawling again, but at a different angle, to bypass the clearing. Flood followed, but turning his head to study the clearing.

It looked like the one he'd come through during his escape from the enemy base. He knew he could be wrong.

Landmark spotting in this kind of brush was a deceptive business. But the timing was right. Judging by how long they'd been crawling, they should be somewhere across the river from the base.

Reaching forward, he tapped Shaw on the ankle. Shaw stopped and looked back at him. Flood pointed to the left. Shaw nodded and continued crawling, but changing direction to circle around the clearing toward the river.

They were almost past it when Shaw abruptly dropped flat to the ground on his belly. Flood imitated him and lay there motionless, listening. It was several seconds before he heard what Shaw had: boots crunching through the brush towards them. Flood turned his head slightly on his folded arms and squinted into the clearing.

An enemy sentry paced into the clearing, carrying a rifle with a bayonet attached. He moved carelessly, and he was alone. But one was all it would take. If the sentry suspected their presence, they were finished. There was no question of taking him by surprise and killing him. A dead or missing sentry would alert the whole base to the fact that an enemy was inside, and end their only hope of accomplishing the mission.

They watched the sentry cross the clearing and enter the trail on the other side. He was strolling along lazily with only token obedience to his job of having a look around him.

Shaw waited a full minute after the sound of the sentry's footsteps died out. Then he rose to his hands and knees and crawled on, with Flood close behind him. They stopped again when they reached a trail, looking into it in both directions and listening. Then they went across it, into the bushes on the other side.

A few minutes later they were into the ferns at the river's edge. Shaw inched forward ahead of Flood, pushing his head through for a look. Peering past him, Flood saw that he'd been right. They were directly across from the enemy base. He could vaguely make out the dark shapes of the moored tanker, the grounded hulk, and the dock, empty now with the four MTBs out on their nightly job of prowling the straits. The high watchtower showed clearly.

He could even make out the two guards at the top of it with their mounted heavy machine gun. The buildings in the camp clearing blended with the dark ground at that distance, but there were obviously more of them than when Flood had escaped.

Shaw suddenly pulled back into the ferns and stretched flat on the ground, pushing Flood down beside him.

A moment later an armed trooper came walking along the river bank from their right. He stopped almost directly in front of them. Seconds later, another armed trooper appeared from the left, joining the first one. They exchanged a few words. A match flared. Cigarettes were lit.

They were obviously on sentry duty, patrolling this bank of the river. And by chance, this happened to be the place where they met. Flood looked at Shaw, waiting for him to pull back further and start circling to find a safer approach to the river. But Shaw didn't move. He stayed where he was, waiting. And Flood had to assume the captain knew what he was doing.

But it was hard. Flood had to cope with the irritating drag of time as he lay there waiting while the two sentries smoked and talked. According to the luminous dial of Shaw's watch, it was a little past two in the morning. Barely three hours left until dawn.

At last the sentries flicked the stubs of their cigarettes into the water. They turned away from each other and separated, pacing off in opposite directions along the river bank.

But even when the sounds they made were gone, Shaw didn't move. He just looked at his watch, and kept looking at it, waiting.

Flood gritted his teeth as more of their precious time was eaten away.

Shaw was still looking at his watch when the sentries came back and met again. Five minutes, it had taken them. Exactly five minutes. That would have to be enough.

Again, the sentries exchanged a few words. But this time they did not smoke. Turning their backs on each other, they went off in opposite directions.

Shaw sat up on the ground. Quickly he got the big square of rubber from his belt and spread it on the ground. Flood did the same, relieved to be doing something, anything. Shaw took the Thompson submachine gun from him and put it down on the rubber. Detaching the spare cartridge magazine from his ammo belt, he placed it on the tommy gun. He wrapped the rubber tightly around both, leaving the weapon's carrying strap outside the wrapping.

When he had the rubber wrapped securely to keep out water, he tightened the strap as far as it would go. Then he hung the wrapped weapon and spare magazine around his neck by the tightened strap. It rested high on the back of his shoulders, exactly where he wanted it.

Flood had already placed the two grenades and two handguns he'd been carrying in the middle of his square of rubber. Shaw added to them his pair of grenades, Nambu automatic, and Enfield .38, plus his flashlight. Flood wrapped the rubber around them to make a tight, water-resistant bundle. He tied the ends of the rubber together so that he could loop the bundle high around his neck, like Shaw's.

Then they pulled off their boots. Getting stones from their pockets, they poured an equal amount into each boot.

Shaw glanced at his watch and went flat to the ground again. Flood stretched out beside him. They waited, motionless.

The sentries returned, met, and separated. As soon as they were gone in their opposite directions, Shaw sat up and looked at his watch.

They had four and a half minutes to get beyond the sentries' line of night vision.

Shaw plucked the small pill bottle from his pocket, unscrewed the cap. Quickly, he spilled two more pills into his palm and popped them in his mouth, swallowing them dry. He got a folded square of paper from his pocket. Flood's drawing of the base layout. Twisting it small, he pushed it inside the bottle. He screwed the top on tightly and put the bottle back in his pocket.

He hadn't offered any pills to Flood.

Flood looked at him. "How often can you take those," he whispered, "before your heart goes?"

"Never mind. Let's go." Shaw picked up his boots and went out of the ferns in a low crouch, wading into the dark river.

Flood went in after him, also carrying his boots. When they were chest-deep in the water, they let the stone-weighted boots sink to the bottom. Then they began swimming across the river, angling toward the grounded hulk in which the male prisoners were kept at night.

They used a slow breaststroke, because it created no splashes and left little wake for anyone to spot. They kept looking back as they swam. When they could make out the sentries pacing toward each other on the bank they'd left, they stopped swimming and began treading water. A stationary object was less likely to be noticed than a moving one.

The sentries met on the river bank. It was impossible to see if they were looking out across the river. Shaw and Flood continued to tread water, only their heads and the rubber-wrapped bundles showing above the surface.

Fortunately, there was little moon at this time of the month, only a thin sliver. *Un*fortunately, there were also very few clouds, and too much starlight.

The sentries remained together for an uncomfortably long period. Finally they separated, pacing away from each other. Shaw watched them go, then tapped Flood's shoulder. They resumed swimming.

When they were halfway across the river, they stopped looking back. But they kept to the slow breaststroke, their anxiety now concentrated on what lay ahead. They couldn't see any night sentries around the hulk or the tanker; but they were undoubtedly there.

They were almost to the hulk when any doubts about it were dispelled. A rifle-carrying trooper appeared on the river side of the hulk's deck.

Shaw and Flood stopped and treaded water again.

A tiny pinpoint of yellow glowed in the dark blur of the enemy trooper's face above. It dimmed, then brightened again. He was having a smoke. Suddenly, he leaned against the rail and looked down at the water.

Flood's heart squeezed. The trooper seemed to be looking straight at them. He tried to sink deeper in the water.

But it became evident that the trooper up there was seeing nothing but his own thoughts. After a while he finished his cigarette and flipped the butt over the rail. It arced down through the air and dropped into the water in front of Flood and Shaw. Near enough for them to hear the brief sizzle as it went out.

Up on the deck above, the trooper turned from the rail and strolled away, out of sight. Shaw and Flood looked at each other. It was a moment before they resumed their swim.

When they reached the side of the grounded hulk, Shaw looked questioningly at Flood. During the day it was possible to see the hole the exploding torpedo had made below the waterline near the keel. But at night the dark surface of the water was impenetrable. Flood had to locate it by memory, swiming alongside the hull until he judged they were directly above the hole. Sucking his lungs full of air, he shut his eyes and began swimming down under the water.

He swam down blindly, feeling his way with his fingertips along the flaking side of the submerged section of the hull. His lungs were beginning to labor, demanding fresh oxygen, when his forearm scraped a jagged point curling up from the top of the hole.

Flood jerked his arm away. What he didn't need at this stage was to slash himself open on the rusting metal edges of that hole. Forcing himself farther down under the water, he very carefully pulled himself through the hole. He swam inside it for three long strokes before letting himself bob to the surface.

As soon as his head was out of the water, he opened his mouth and gulped in air. His eyes snapped open and saw nothing but total blackness. Fumbling with the rubber bundle around his neck, he pried it open just enough to reach in and find the flashlight. Pulling it out, he snapped it on.

Shaw had bobbed to the surface near him. He blinked against the sudden glare as Flood flashed the light around them, treading water.

They were in the ruined, half-flooded engine room of the hulk. The boilers had blown apart, adding to the havoc created by the explosion of the torpedo. All of the massive machinery was mangled. But what concerned Flood was the destruction of all the ladders that had led out of the engine room. There was no way left for them to reach the upper decks from here.

Flood switched the flashlight lower and located the shaft tunnel. It was half-filled with water. But only half. He swam toward it, propelling himself with his legs and left arm, holding the flashlight above the surface with his right hand.

Shaw followed him silently. It was now Flood's turn to lead. He was the one who knew the anatomy of ships.

Flood hauled himself into the shaft tunnel and started making his way through it, shining the flashlight ahead of him. Shaw stayed close behind him as they worked through the tight confines of the tunnel, along the twisted propeller shaft.

Flood stopped when he found what he was looking for. They were at the bottom of a narrow vertical shaft. He shined the light up into it. The iron ladder was intact. Sticking the flashlight in his shirt pocket so its beam still shined upwards, he straightened up inside the vertical shaft and got hold of the ladder. He began to climb, dripping water on Shaw, who was hauling himself up below him.

The shaft opened into a narrow passageway between decks. Flood got the flashlight from his pocket and led the way along it. Their bare feet made little sound as they went.

Shaw stuck close to Flood as they worked their way through the lower guts of the old freighter. They turned into so many different shafts, tunnels, and passageways that Shaw soon lost all sense of direction. It was like being in a confined maze. But Flood never paused. He seemed to know where they were going.

He did. Though Shaw didn't realize it, they had reached the forward part of the hulk. Flood turned into a narrow, low passageway that led toward the bow. They were half-way along it when boots rang sharply on the deck inches above their heads.

Shaw froze. In front of him the flashlight in Flood's hand snapped off. The sharp sounds of the boots above them marched on past, striding quickly. Shaw and Flood crouched silently in pitch-black darkness. Two pairs of boots sounded, running across the deck just above their heads in the opposite direction.

The two men in the darkness listened to the sounds receding. They waited, not moving. Perhaps a minute and a half passed. There were no more sounds. Flood switched the flashlight on.

Shaw looked at his face, saw it going slack with slow release from the sudden, clutching fear. He pointed to the flashlight; it was getting dimmer. Flood nodded, pulling himself together. He led the way swiftly through the rest of the passage, but treading carefully with his bare feet to make no noise.

In the coastwatcher shack, it was still dark when Nora woke. But when she lit the small coconut-oil lamp and looked at her watch, she saw her mental clock had been working perfectly while she slept. It was three-thirty in the morning. She was still tired; but this was as much rest as they could allow themselves.

She got into her boots and woke Qualey. "Get up. It'll be dawn soon."

He blinked at her in sleepy confusion for a moment. Then he remembered. He stumbled to his feet quickly, without grumbling.

"Make us some coffee, will you?" he pleaded thickly. "A lot of it. Hot, black, and strong."

He knew better than she did how much work they'd have to do to get the *Skylark* repaired enough to take off. And he knew how close a thing it was going to be; whether they would be able to get it fixed in time or not.

TWELVE

Flood and Shaw had reached their goal; they were inside the aft section of the forward cargo hold. Flood played the beam of the flashlight along the bottom of the bulkhead dividing this part of the hold from the section containing the male prisoners. He found what he was looking for: the dogged-down iron hatch connecting the two sections of the hold. On the other side their captors had hacked away the means of opening it. They hadn't bothered with this side.

Giving Shaw the flashlight to hold, Flood went to work on the upper securing lock. It was stuck with rust. Bracing his legs apart, Flood pulled at it with both hands, getting all his weight and the strength of his shoulders and back into the pull. For several seconds the lock didn't budge. When it did, it came open all at once, with a loud scraping creak.

Both men involuntarily looked up at the hatch cover over this part of the hold. They listened for several moments. There were no sounds from above to indicate that

133

the noise had carried enough to alarm the enemy guards on the main deck.

Flood crouched and took hold of the lower securing lock. He worked at it more carefully, with short, sharp, vigorous tugs. Just enough to finally break the rust formation that froze it in position. Then he slowly eased the lock the rest of the way, getting it done with a minimum of noise. Straightening, he shoved the connecting hatch open.

They were all bunched on the other side, wakened by the noise he'd made, blinking into the sudden glare of the flashlight. All of them. Flood made the quick tally with a surge of relief: Sergeant Leary, Private Soames and the other seven troopers, Tengal, the Dutchman and his son, the American oil driller, and the Eurasian planter.

Leary stared at Flood as he stepped through to them. "You made it. . . ." It came as a simple statement, not an exclamation.

"Looks like." Flood jerked a thumb at Shaw as he came in after him. "This is Captain Shaw."

Soames, the big Australian private, was grinning at them. "Beautiful. How many've the boys you bring with you, Captain?"

Flood gave them the bad news: "He's it. All of it."

Leary frowned at Shaw, puzzled. "Excuse me, Captain, but I don't get this. . . ."

"What's the difference," one of the American privates growled. "We're sprung. We get out the way they got in."

But the Dutchman already understood the hitch: "What about the women and the children?"

Shaw nodded. "That's the problem. One of them. I'm afraid you all have to remain here. The escape is set for late tomorrow, when the women and children can be included in it."

"The hell you say," the American private snapped, starting for the opened hatch. "I'm getting out *now*."

Sergeant Leary put an arm like a rigid bar of iron across the private's chest, stopping him. "You try, and I'm going to break your neck." The way he said the words, they were not just a figure of speech.

The hulking Soames stepped in front of the private. "And I'll help him."

The private backed away from them and threw a pleading look at Shaw. "But Captain, if you're the only one they sent to help us . . ."

"We've got a plane too," Flood said dryly. "A bomber. Sort of."

Leary shook his head, confused. "I guess I still don't get it."

"Then you'd better listen very carefully," Shaw told him, "while I explain." He sat down on the metal floor of the cargo hold, putting the dimming flashlight down carefully in front of his bent knees.

As the other men gathered around him, Flood looked them over. They were all in worse shape than when he'd left; much thinner, drained of energy, their eyes feverish.

"The women and kids . . ." he asked Soames ". . . are they all right?"

"Mrs. Burns ain't good. She's been going downhill fast since they shot her husband. The rest are okay. Except for dysentery. We've all got that."

"What about that Filipino nurse?"

Soames shot him a thoughtful look. "Esther? She's why we ain't in worse shape. No malaria. She gets pills for us from the camp's commander, in exchange for doctoring his men."

"Pay attention," Shaw snapped. He had gotten the twist of paper from the pill bottle. Opening it, he smoothed it out on the metal flooring, with the flashlight shining on it. He took a stubby pencil from his pocket.

"Now, this is the layout of this base, as Flood remembered it. Have there been any additions or changes?"

Sergeant Leary crouched beside him. "We've built more personnel shelters." He took the pencil from Shaw and marked them on the layout sketch. "And we're building two more now, on the other side of the watchtower and feeding area. For the officers and crews of the torpedo boats." He added these to the layout.

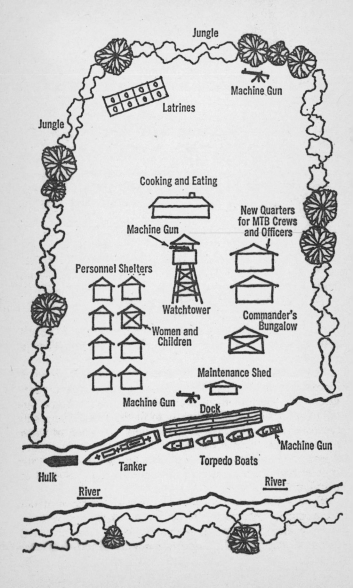

SAM FLOOD'S SKETCH:
LAYOUT OF ENEMY BASE

Jungle

Machine Gun

Latrines

Jungle

Cooking and Eating

New Quarters
for MTB Crews
and Officers

Machine Gun

Personnel Shelters

Watchtower

Commander's
Bungalow

Women and
Children

Maintenance Shed

Machine Gun

Dock

Machine Gun

Tanker

Torpedo Boats

Hulk

River

River

"Is that where you'll be working tomorrow? *Late* tomorrow, that's the important point."

Leary nodded. "You can count on it, Captain. Take us all day to finish 'em."

"Where are the women and children kept?"

"They stick to this shelter, pretty much." Leary marked it.

"What about the positions of the heavy machine guns? Have they been changed? Are there any more?"

Sergeant Leary looked at the three machine gun positions Flood had marked on his sketch: the one on the watch tower, the one beside the dock and maintenance shed, the one that was manned on the end MTB during the day.

"These are the same. But we got one more, on the edge of the clearing near the latrines." Leary marked it on the sketch.

"None on the tanker or this ship?" Shaw asked him.

"No. Those're all."

"Any more enemy troops been added since Flood left?"

"Only two. They showed up with a little motorboat. They're using it to patrol the river."

"We know about it," Flood said sourly.

"Where does it dock?" Shaw asked.

"It doesn't," Leary told him. "Only comes in to refuel and change men. Rest of the time it's away, prowling up the river."

Shaw studied the map in silence for several seconds. Then he looked up and began speaking in a clipped, precise voice. He told them about the plan he'd worked out with Flood, adjusting it slightly to fit the latest changes in the base camp. He went into the part that each of them would have to play in the operation, and the timing. Once it started, everything would have to be accomplished with split-second precision if it was to have any chance at all of working.

They asked questions, and he answered them in detail —but quickly. The flashlight was rapidly dimming.

He explained about the plane and what it was expected to accomplish when it came. He didn't mention what he knew as well as Qualey: the *Skylark* might not make it in time.

Flood had removed the rubber bundle from around his neck and set it on the floor. Shaw opened it up, revealing the four grenades and four handguns. He took one of the grenades and gave it to Flood, then looked at Leary.

"Sergeant, you know these men. Assign the rest of these as you think best."

Leary picked up the Colt .45 automatic with a tight grin, fondling it.

Flood looked at the expressions of the other men staring at the weapons. Excitement at the prospect of striking back at their captors at last was combating their fear of what the coming day held for them. The Dutchman had one arm tightly around his son, but his face was eager.

Leary stuck the .45 out of sight inside his shirt, along with one of the grenades. He picked up the two remaining grenades, looking at the other men thoughtfully. One he gave to a Dutch soldier. He held the other, cocked an eye at the American private who'd wanted to leave—and tossed it to him.

The man caught the grenade with both hands and suddenly grinned. "Okay, Sarge . . ." He slipped the grenade inside his shirt, and pushed it around to the small of his back above his belt, where the bulge wouldn't be noticeable.

Leary gave Shaw's Enfield .38 to Soames, and one of the Nambu automatics to a British trooper. He hesitated over the other one, glancing at the Dutchman.

The Dutchman shook his head. "With a rifle, I am an expert marksman. But I have not had practice with pistols."

"We'll see to it you get a rifle, when the time comes," Leary told him. He gave the remaining Nambu automatic to the oil driller and looked to Shaw. "We can work out which of us does what in the dark. You'd better get out while you can. Your flashlight's ready to go dead."

Shaw nodded, stuck the layout sketch in his pocket, and stood up with the flashlight. It was only giving off a fitful glow now. "And it's almost dawn. Remember, don't move until the time we've set. One hour before dark. If any of you give it away before then, it'll destroy everything. And get all of us killed."

"Okay, Captain," Leary said. "Got you the first time."

"I'm depending on that, Sergeant." Shaw started out through the opened hatch.

Floor wrapped his grenade in rubber and tied it around his neck again as he followed. He paused in the hatchway, looking back at the prisoners. He gave Soames and Leary a mock salute. "Good luck. . . ."

Soames smiled crookedly and returned the mocking salute.

Leary just looked at Flood soberly. "Sure. You too."

Flood stepped through into the other section of the forward hold and closed the hatch. He shoved the securing locks back in place, sealing the prisoners inside again. Then he took the flashlight from Shaw and swiftly led the way across the bottom of the cargo hold.

The flashlight gave out entirely before they were halfway through the bowels of the hulk.

In the sudden darkness, Flood stopped and stuck the flashlight in his pocket. "Hang onto my belt," he whispered.

Shaw grasped the back of Flood's belt with his right hand. Even that close, he couldn't see Flood's back. He was tugged along as Flood moved forward again, more slowly now.

They followed the twists and turns of the return route through utter blackness; Flood finding the way blindly, depending entirely on feel and memory. But Shaw was not surprised when they finally descended an iron ladder and he felt the propeller shaft against his legs.

They crawled the length of the tunnel, into the engine room. Still totally blind in the darkness, they swam across it together, until their outreaching hands found the inside of the hull. Taking deep breaths, they swam down underwater, feeling for the torpedo hole. They reached it at last and swam through.

When they bobbed to the surface of the river, the sudden starlight seemed terribly bright. And there was a tinge of gray streaking the night sky on the horizon, a prelude to dawn. There were perhaps ten minutes left before they would be caught out in the open in the first light of day.

Treading water, they looked around quickly for sentries. But they couldn't locate any of them in that first scan, and there was no time left to spend on searching for them. They began swimming in the direction of the empty dock, using the slow, quiet breaststroke.

They were making their way around the side of the tanker's hull when the motorboat came chugging downriver towards the base, its searchlight stabbing ahead of it.

Shaw and Flood swam faster, as fast as they could without making noise. There were sudden sounds of activity on the tanker's deck above them. In the camp, someone was snapping orders. The motorboat came swiftly into the base with its searchlight swinging, reaching out for the heads of the two men in the water.

They reached the dock as the river patrol boat behind them came past the stranded hulk. Quickly, they swam in under the dock and found the soft river bottom with their feet. Crouching so low their faces were almost touching the surface of the water, Shaw and Flood moved in deeper under the dock, until they were against the slope of the muddy bank.

They lowered themselves down carefully in sitting position, waist deep in the water. Leaning against the mud of the bank, they stared out under the dock at the river beyond.

The motorboat bumped against the dock in front of them two seconds later, the motor switching off. They listened to the sounds of the mooring lines being attached, and the six troopers climbing out of it. As they marched off into the camp, their boots stamped on the dock inches above the heads of the two hidden men.

Moments later, another six pairs of boots thudded onto the dock above them. The replacement crew. Flood and Shaw watched the motorboat sink deeper in the water as the men climbed into it.

They listened to words being exchanged in sleepy voices, and the sounds of the outboard engine being refueled. Then the lines were cast off, and the engine started up again.

Flood and Shaw watched the motorboat chug away from the dock, heading back upriver. It left ripples behind which reached under the dock and lapped the waists of the two men. Beyond the dock, the surface of the river was beginning to shine with the light of dawn.

Flood and Shaw leaned against the mud under the dock and looked at each other in silence. A long wait stretched ahead of them. They were going to have to remain hidden here, not moving, for the entire day.

Nora Ferguson and Phil Qualey were also in the water at that moment. They were in the mountain creek up to their necks, working with hammer and screwdriver, trying to get the caved-in forward section of the left pontoon pried off.

The pontoons were constructed of a number of sealed, separate, water-tight compartments. Fortunately, only the first compartment had been damaged. If they could get it off and hammer the smashed-in aluminum nose into some semblance of its former shape, they could then do something about resealing it. Unfortunately, it was years since it had been last taken apart; the securing bolts were frozen with rust.

Qualey had managed, by using every bit of strength in his body, to get most of them unstuck and unscrewed. But this one wouldn't budge. The only thing left was to try to break it off.

Nora held the screwdriver in place with both hands, trying to force the bit under the frozen bolt while Qualey slammed at the handle with the hammer.

"That's not doing it," Nora told him. "You've got to hit *harder*."

"I'm afraid of missing. I could smash your hand with this thing."

"I'm willing to chance it. Come *on*."

Qualey worriedly grasped the hammer with both hands, took very careful aim, and slugged the handle end of the screwdriver as hard as he could.

"That's it!" Nora exulted. "It's going under! Try it again!"

Qualey drew a deep breath, drew the hammer back, and smashed it against the end of the screwdriver.

Something broke that time. But it wasn't the frozen bolt. Nora stared at the half of the screwdriver she held in her stinging hands. Qualey glowered at the stub of the snapped-off bit still stuck under the bolt.

"Oh sweet Jesus . . ." he groaned.

"You said you had a spare in the plane," Nora reminded him.

"I *think* I do. . . ." With a sigh, Qualey dragged himself up out of the water, on top of the pontoon.

Climbing in the open cabin door, he made his way back in the plane, dripping water as he went. Reaching the tail, he had to get down on the floor and snake the rest of the way to the tool kit.

He had to rummage through it awhile before he found the screwdriver. As an afterthought, he also took a chisel with him. Snaking backward, he made his way out of the *Skylark* and dropped into the water with Nora.

They went back to work on the frozen bolt.

The lieutenant in charge of the searching party in the mountains stood eyeing the marker that Nora had put on her husband's grave. He was remembering the man his patrol had killed very near this spot less than two weeks earlier.

He hadn't known the dead man's name was Ferguson, of course. But it didn't take much thought to put it together. The body was no longer where it had been left, and this was a fresh grave.

After they'd killed the man, the lieutenant had assumed he'd been a lone refugee trying to flee the country. But obviously that had been wrong. He'd had friends nearby. *Somebody* had buried him.

The lieutenant made a reconnaissance of the various trails leading from the area. One of them, leading up the slope, appeared to have been used quite recently. The lieutenant started up this trail with his men.

After about a mile, the trail ran into several other trails, and there were no longer any signs to show which one the people who had buried the dead man had taken.

The lieutenant stopped to consider the possibilities. Finally, he made a decision and spread his men out to either side of him through the heavy brush—as far apart as they could get and still maintain contact with each other. When the line was fanned all the way out, the men at the ends of it were a mile apart.

They moved straight up the side of the mountain, sweeping it for signs of the enemy they were after.

tions, Inc., P.O. Box 1014, Greenwich, Connecticut 06830. Please order by number and title. Catalog available on request.

THIRTEEN

With the full light of dawn casting long shadows across the MTB base, the camp's normal day of activity began. On the grounded hulk the deck hatch covering the forward hold was unclamped and opened. The cargo net was lowered to the prisoners at the bottom. The men climbed it to the main deck where their armed guards awaited them.

There were more guards than when Flood had managed his escape; four of them on the deck, and four more waiting for them when they came down the gangway to the ground. The guards held their semiautomatic rifles ready and watched the prisoners closely. But none of them noticed any sign of the grenades and pistols that six of the fourteen male prisoners were carrying concealed in their clothing.

On top of the watchtower, the two troopers manning the heavy mounted machine gun looked down at the prisoners being marched tamely across the camp clearing to the cooking shelter. There was nothing about the way they moved between their armed guards to indicate that they were no longer tame.

Esther and Mrs. Ruyter were already at the cook shelter with the two Ruyter children. Mrs. Burns hadn't felt strong enough to come out of their shelter for the past two days. Esther had gotten the camp commander's permission to take Mrs. Burns her meals. It was the same unvarying diet both morning and evening: tea, fish, and rice.

The men lined up with them to get their breakfast, which they had exactly five minutes to finish. As they exchanged good morning's with the two women and children, and asked after the health of Mrs. Burns, the four armed guards spread out to watch them. There was nothing inattentive in their scrutiny. The commander of the camp had made it plain to his men that if there was another escape, it would not only be the remaining prisoners who would suffer for it.

Sergeant Leary was second in line for his morning rations. His tin cup was filled with steaming tea, and the mixture of fish and rice was ladled into his tin bowl. Carrying them, he drifted over beside Esther. He took a long swallow of tea and then whispered to her.

She stiffened, staring at him. Her startled reaction was quickly hidden; but not quickly enough. One of the armed guards turned his head to look straight at them, his eyes narrowing a bit.

Leary resumed eating. So did Esther. When he had half of his fish and rice finished, Leary washed it down with a swallow of tea and looked at Esther again.

"I think I'm coming down with something," he told her in a loud voice. "My throat feels all raw, and it's hard to swallow this stuff."

Esther put down her bowl and turned to him with an expression of professional concern. "Let me have a look. Open your mouth and stick out your tongue."

Leary did so. Esther looked into his mouth for a moment.

"Now close your mouth." She moved closer to feel his throat for swollen glands.

Leary whispered to her without moving his lips. Esther's fingers moved on his throat, her hands concealing its movement as he whispered.

The guard was watching them again, suspiciously. He began drifting closer.

Leary stopped whispering.

Esther dropped her hands and said in a normal tone: "There's no swelling. Your throat is a little red, but I don't think it's anything serious. Let me know this evening if it's still bothering you or getting worse."

Leary nodded matter-of-factly. "Okay. Thanks."

He went back to eating, wolfing the rest of the food and washing it down with the last of his tea just as the guards began barking orders at them. The breakfast period was over.

The male prisoners were lined up and marched off to begin their day of working on the partially constructed shelters for the officers and crews of the torpedo boats.

There were two of them, and they were to be bigger and more complete than the camp's personnel shelters. One already had a roof on it; the other was still only a raised platform and support poles. The armed guards fanned out to watch the male prisoners go to work putting thatched siding on the one with the roof.

As they began work, Sergeant Leary glanced back across the clearing. Esther was walking towards the small shelter carrying Mrs. Burns's breakfast to her, followed by Mrs. Ruyter and her children.

He just hoped she had understood exactly what he had told her to do.

The four MTBs returned to the base a short time later. As they docked, the camp commander came out onto the veranda of his bungalow. He noted with surprise, as he automatically looked them over, that each of the MTBs still had its two torpedo tubes armed with torpedoes. The commander stood where he was, waiting to find out why.

The crews of the torpedo boats tramped across the dock and headed for their temporary quarters on the top deck of the grounded hulk. They were replaced by only two men, who took up their day's station at one of the two machine guns on the last MTB in line.

The chief officer of each MTB marched to the bungalow, coming to stiff attention and saluting the commander. He returned their salute and led them inside to make their regular morning report on the previous night's activities.

This report turned out to be different from any in the past. The reason all the tubes were still armed was that there had been nothing to fire the torpedoes at. For the first night since the base had been established, the four MTBs had not been able to spot a single enemy escape vessel trying to slip south through the Vitiaz Straits.

It was strange. Very strange.

Leaving the commander to mull over the significance of their report, the four officers went off to get a day's sleep in their temporary quarters, an officer's cabin on the tanker.

Alone, the commander puzzled for some time over various possible reasons for the lack of activity last night in the straits. One explanation could be that the Allied vessels to the north had finally realized the futility of trying to get through; that they were taking the safer course of waiting where they were to be captured. But there could be other explanations. . . .

A glance at his watch reminded him that fortunately the job of choosing from among the many possible reasons was not his responsibility. His duties did not go beyond running this base properly. He got up and went to the radio room. It was time to pass on the morning report to his superiors in Rabaul. Understanding the significance of this morning's odd report was *their* responsibility.

Sam Flood sat in the water huddled against the mud bank under the dock, listening to the torpedo boats being refueled by the long hose from the tanker.

He was wearing Shaw's watch. Beside him, Shaw lay against the mud, sound asleep. He had lost more blood, the wound in his side having come open with all the swimming. The flesh of his face had sunk to the bones, and even while he slept his exhaustion showed.

But at exactly noon Flood was going to have to wake him, so he could take his own turn at sleeping. He needed it. It required steady effort for him to stay awake. His whole body ached, and his head buzzed with weariness.

Stoically, he continued to stare at the sleek lines of the four MTB hulls with tired, burning eyes, waiting out the hours of the long morning.

Qualey was tired too. He sat on the ground hammering at the inside of the detached forward compartment of the *Skylark's* left pontoon, pounding out the deep dents in its nose. His arms were getting heavy to lift, and his nerves were jumpy from lack of sleep.

Nora sat beside him watching. On the ground beside her, the canvas, dope, and tape that would be needed for sealing lay waiting.

Qualey paused to wipe the pouring sweat from his forehead and eyes. He was panting in the sticky heat.

Nora looked at his face. "Can I help?"

He sighed and shook his head. "It's a one man job." His voice was weak and weary.

"Then let me do it for awhile," she told him decisively. "I've got the idea now."

Qualey hesitated and then gratefully handed over the hammer to her.

As she took up the pounding, he got to his feet and stretched to ease the cramped ache in his lower back. He yawned, scratched himself, and gazed sleepily at his battered old seaplane.

That made him remember the promise Captain Shaw had made to him. For a time, Qualey luxuriated in the thought of it: a brand new plane. Two engines. Six passengers. A whole new career ahead of him.

And if he handled it right, that needn't be all. It was sure going to make a welcome change in his life, having a rich friend who was obligated to him. He smiled to himself, stretched again, and turned back to Nora.

Squatting, he took the hammer from her and returned to work with renewed enthusiasm.

On the platform of their shelter in the base camp, Esther and Mrs. Ruyter sat on either side of Mrs. Burns, talking to her softly and urgently while the Ruyter children squatted close by, watching with solemn, fearful eyes.

Mrs. Burns lay on her straw mat and rolled her head listlessly at them.

"I wouldn't be able to do it, dear." Her voice was trembly and disinterested. "I'm so weak I can't even stand up for long."

"I'll help you," Esther told her determinedly. "I'll keep my arm around you, and you can lean on me all the way."

Mrs. Burns tried to smile at her. It was a weak smile. "I'll only slow you down. Just leave me here. I really don't care much anyway."

"But don't you understand?" Mrs. Ruyter demanded angrily. "The men *won't* just leave you!"

Esther nodded. "That's the point. If you try to stay behind here, they'll come back to carry you out. *That* will slow everyone down. You'll get some of them killed that way."

Mrs. Burns stared up at them, digesting this. "I . . . don't want to bring harm to anyone else. . . ." she said weakly.

"Then you've got to *try*."

Mrs. Burns sighed. It was a long, broken, weary sigh. "All right . . . I'll do my best. . . ."

Mrs. Ruyter broke into a smile of relief. "Good."

"Now please let me sleep. Wake me when it's time. . . ."

"No," Esther said tightly. "You have to start trying *now*. Get your legs working again. Or they'll collapse under you when the time comes."

Mrs. Burns closed her eyes. For a frightened moment, the other two women crouching over her thought she had passed out. But then her eyes opened, and she struggled up on one elbow.

"You'll have to help me, I'm afraid. . . ."

Esther and Mrs. Ruyter got her to her feet. Holding her

up between them, they began walking her back and forth within their shelter.

The children watched, thoughtfully.

It was noon. Flood unstrapped the watch from his wrist and shook Shaw's shoulder, ready to clamp a hand over his mouth if he cried out on waking.

But Shaw woke without a sound. His eyes snapped open and stared at Flood as he took a couple seconds to reorient himself. Then he sat up straighter in the water and nodded, taking the watch from Flood and strapping it on his own wrist.

Flood sagged wearily against the mud of the river bank and closed his eyes. Sleep came in a rush, and he let it engulf him.

Shaw looked at the rough planks of the dock inches above him, and at the hulls of the MTBs walling off his view of the river. His mind was still half dazed with sleep, and he couldn't seem to come all the way out of it. The whole of his injured side was throbbing with pain now, from shoulder to hip. A fever was spreading from the wound through his blood system. His arms and legs felt heavy and limp.

He shook his head to clear away the fog. It wouldn't clear. Taking the small bottle from his pocket, he looked at it hesitantly. Then he took one pill from it and put it in his mouth. Quietly unscrewing his canteen, he washed down the pill and slaked his parched throat with three long swallows of water.

Then he just sat there beside the sleeping Flood, and waited.

An hour later it began to rain. It began as it usually did in the tropics, all at once and in full force; pouring down in a solid, battering deluge that left little air to breathe.

In the camp clearing, the four armed guards supervising the male prisoners ducked into the shelter of the roofed building they were constructing. At first, they tried to keep the prisoners working out in the rain. But they soon gave that up, because it proved impossible to see all the prisoners through the thick downpour. They were forced to let them come in under the protection of the thatched roof.

Soaking wet, the prisoners sat together shivering on one side of the platform. The four guards squatted on the other side, watching them and nervously fingering their weapons.

Across the clearing, Esther and Mrs. Ruyter interrupted Mrs. Burns's half-hour rest. Hauling her to her feet again, they resumed walking her back and forth across the platform of their shelter. The children stood at the edge of the platform, staring at the rain outside. It came down past the edge of the roof like a solid curtain, churning the ground to mud and making it impossible to see the rest of the camp through it.

The sudden rain brought a certain amount of refreshing coolness with it into the steaming tropic heat. But Shaw, huddled under the dock with the sleeping Flood, felt no sense of relief from it. He was thinking of the *Skylark*. If the rain continued like this, it would be impossible for the plane to take off, let alone get here on time to do its job.

Unrelenting, the rain continued to drum thunderously on the dock over Shaw's head. Water dripped down between the planks and spattered his hat and canvas poncho. Beside him, Flood slept with his head tipped back. Big drops of water began hitting the mosquito netting covering his face. His eyes blinked open, startled. But when he realized what it was, he just rolled his head to one side in the mud and went back to sleep.

Shaw continued to sit there, shivering slightly as the water dripped on him. The unvarying drumming of the rain on the dock stuffed his ears, blocking out all other sound. He began praying for the rain to stop. And he fervently nursed the possibility that this was only a local downpour, and that it might not be raining at all, up in the mountains where the plane was. . . .

It *was* raining in the mountains. But Qualey and Nora were quite comfortable by now, inside the *Skylark*'s cabin. As the rain beat on the wings and slashed at the windows, they continued to work single-mindedly on the damaged nose of the pontoon.

They had pounded out the dents until it was now a reasonable semblance of its former shape. But there were big open cracks in the aluminum; these had to be sealed, or the nose of the pontoon would fill with water and sink when they tried to take off. They were trying to seal the cracks with the only method available to them. They had stretched canvas over the aluminum, taping it down tightly. Now they were swabbing the canvas with dope.

The dope was an efficient sealing agent. The only trouble was, Qualey didn't have enough of it in the plane to do this big a job efficiently. The little they had, they were forced to spread too thinly. Which wasn't the sort of waterproofing job that could be expected to last long, if it worked at all.

But it didn't *have* to last long. Qualey just hoped it would work long enough for him to fly the plane up out of this stream.

At the moment the search party led by the lieutenant was only one mile below Nora and Qualey, sheltering under a dense cluster of trees on the forested mountain slope.

In spite of the thick overhang of tree foliage, they were all wet and miserable. Too much of the heavy rain was leaking through on them. The lieutenant leaned against a tree trunk in his damp, clinging uniform and took a jaundiced view of further searching. Even if the enemy had left any signs of their going nearby, this rain would wipe them out. And besides, it was getting late in the day and they were far from home.

He came to the conclusion that after the rain stopped they would make just one more token sweep of the area, and then head back to their base.

They would make that final sweep, he decided, a little higher up the slope.

It was late afternoon when the rain finally stopped. In the MTB base camp, the four armed guards snapped orders at the male prisoners, prodding them with the points of their bayonets. The men began climbing off the sheltered platform to resume their work under the watchful eyes of the guards.

The oil driller, jumping off the platform, slipped in the fresh mud. He stumbled, bending forward as he tried to regain his balance.

The Nambu automatic fell out of his shirt.

Frantically, the oil driller threw himself down flat in the mud on top of it, covering it with his body.

Sergeant Leary and the other men held their breaths as they watched a narrow-eyed guard step towards the oil driller, raising his rifle.

Desperately, his heart thudding, the oil driller fumbled under him with both hands, trying to make it look as though he were having trouble getting up.

The guard jabbed him in the hip with his bayonet, yelling at him to get up.

The oil driller stumbled to his feet, floundering in the mud, more mud caking his face and clothes.

The pistol was once more concealed inside his shirt.

"I tripped," he mumbled, and tried an insane grin.

The guard was unimpressed. He motioned with the rifle, growling at him to get to work.

None of the guards had seen the gun.

The final sweep of the lieutenant's searching party led them straight to the Ferguson coastwatcher shack. Stationing his men around it, the lieutenant went inside with two of them to have a look around. What he found made it obvious that people had used it recently. Very recently.

With a surge of excitement, the lieutenant realized his quarry must be close by. They weren't in the area he had just combed through. Which left three possible directions.

Striding out of the shack, the lieutenant divided up his men. A small nucleus he kept with him guarding the shack. One group he sent to comb through the higher slopes, and another he sent straight ahead along the slope.

The last group headed down the slope, towards the creek where Qualey and Nora were at work repairing the *Skylark*.

FOURTEEN

Shaw looked at his watch. In an hour and a half it would be dusk. He hunched forward, listening to the maintenance crews getting the torpedo boats ready for the coming night. In the interval after the maintenance men left and before the regular crews came aboard, they would strike.

There was a cold glitter in Shaw's eyes. They were no longer feverish. He felt light-headed, but his brain was functioning sharply. His whole body was taut and ready, without a trace of the weariness. That was all the pills he'd taken. His nerve ends were quivering, and his heart was thudding too fast. That was the pills too; but it couldn't be helped. Very soon it would all be over.

He turned his head and looked at Flood lying against the mud of the bank, still apparently asleep. Shaw nudged his arm. Flood instantly opened his eyes, wide-awake. Without turning his head, he slid his eyes toward Shaw.

Shaw held up his watch. Flood squinted at it, then sat

up straight. Shaw tilted two pills into his palm and held them out. Flood hesitated; then took only one of them.

As Shaw put the bottle away, Flood unwrapped his single grenade. Shaw stripped the rubber wrapping from his submachine gun and extra magazine. Flood took the magazine from him and held it in one hand, the grenade in his other hand. Shaw leaned forward and rested the tommy gun across his raised knees.

The two of them waited under the dock, keeping their eyes on the minute hand of Shaw's watch.

With the plane or without it, in exactly fifteen minutes it would be time.

Qualey and Nora got the patched forward compartment of the pontoon fastened in place. Only three of the bolts had been usable. In the other bolt-holes Qualey used chunks of bailing wire.

It was shaky and far from watertight. But it would have to do.

Water poured from them as they climbed out of the stream onto the solid midsection of the pontoon. The cabin door was open, with the drums of spare gasoline waiting just inside. Qualey hauled himself up above the cabin, on top of the wings. Kneeling, he unscrewed the cap of the gas tank.

Nora reached through the cabin door, got the funnel, and handed it up to him. Qualey stuck it in the tank. Then Nora dragged one of the full gasoline drums out and lifted it as much as she could. Qualey reached down with both hands and pulled it up onto the wing with him. Opening it, he began pouring the gasoline through the funnel into the gas tank.

They were both nerved-up by the time urgency. If they didn't take off in the next few minutes, they might as well forget it. They worked as fast as the funnel would take gasoline without slopping over, Nora dragging another drum out each time Qualey tossed an empty away onto the stream bank. But it seemed to take a terribly long time before the tank was finally full.

Qualey screwed the cap back and scrambled down onto

the bank with Nora. Hastily they untied the lines from the plane to the tree trunks. Qualey climbed into the plane while Nora remained on the bank, feet braced apart, hanging onto one of the lines to keep the *Skylark* pointing upstream. Going against the stream's current, it would be able to lift off in a shorter space.

If it ever did lift off.

Qualey stepped over the pile of hand grenades and two rifles, and settled into his pilot's seat at the controls. With a darting movement of his hand, he switched on; first the right magneto. It sputtered—and died.

Cursing, Qualey flicked the switch to *Off*, then back to *Right Magneto*. It coughed; and then caught immediately. Quickly, he flipped the switch to the left magneto. It started with no trouble at all. With a relieved grin, Qualey switched to *Both*. The engine settled into a reassuring roar, the prop spinning into a blur, the *Skylark* tugging at the line.

Qualey turned his head to shout at Nora to drop it and jump in.

His shout turned into a warning shriek as he saw the first of the enemy troopers coming out of the forest towards them.

Nora turned her head and saw three of them, just emerging from the brush, whipping up their rifles. Dropping the line, she went up onto the pontoon and hurled herself through the open cabin door in a frenzied burst of speed. The hard, flat reports of rifles sounded behind her. Bullets slashed past her head and ripped into the wing. She landed on her hands and knees inside the cabin and instantly reached back and slammed the door shut. Rifle shots thudded against the door and whistled through its open window.

Qualey was already gunning the *Skylark* into the stream. "If those bastards hit the engine! ..."

Nora snatched up one of the rifles as she flung herself into a wicker seat. She poked the rifle out the open window as a bullet drilled through the windshield and whispered through the air between them. It left a large hole in the glass with a spiderweb of cracks around it.

There were five enemy troopers out there now, running toward the stream as they fired. Nora began slamming shot after shot at them, not taking time to aim, just flinging the shots in their general direction and firing as fast as she could.

None of her bullets hit any of them. But they kicked up dirt around them and had the next best effect. They twisted away and ran for cover, bringing a momentary lull in the bullets aimed at the moving plane.

With its engine roaring deafeningly and the fuselage shaking with vibration, the *Skylark* raced upstream. But as it gathered speed, Qualey had to fight a new tendency of the plane to swerve to the left. The repaired pontoon was leaking, dragging in the water. His mouth a thin hard line, Qualey opened the throttle all the way and worked the controls with all the skill at his command.

The enemy troopers were firing now from behind cover, and there were more of them. Bullets thudded into the fuselage, whined through the cabin. Nora and Qualey ducked instinctively, Qualey keeping his head up just high enough to see the narrowing way ahead, Nora crouching lower and watching the jungle whip past on either side, terribly close.

A bullet ripped through her hair and tore a notch out of the top of Qualey's ear. He screamed and jerked with the pain, briefly loosening his hold on the controls.

The *Skylark* abruptly swung to the left. It almost snagged a wingtip in the branches of a tree before Qualey fought it back into midstream.

With blood streaming down from his ripped ear, Qualey throttled to top speed. The bottoms of the pontoons were up on the surface of the water now, skimming it. But there was a sharp bend in the stream dead ahead, perilously close. Grimly, Qualey kept his eyes on the nearing bend and pulled the stick back as far as it would go.

The nose came up, the pontoons lifting off the water. Rifles blasted below them as the *Skylark* winged into the air, clearing the tree tops. And then they were out of range.

Circling skyward, Qualey put a hand to his bleeding ear

and looked at Nora. The way she looked back at him made him forget the ear in a sudden surge of pride.

"All in a day's work," he growled, and gave her an almost shamefaced grin.

Nora drew a deep breath and leaned back in the wicker seat, shaking her head slowly as the terror ebbed.

Qualey turned the *Skylark* in the direction of the torpedo-boat base and dropped down, flying between the mountains as low as he could, to minimize the chance of being spotted before they got there.

In the camp clearing, the prisoners were finishing their supper under the watchful eyes of the four rifle-armed guards. In a minute their meal period would be over, and the guards would march the men back to the hulk to be locked up for the night.

It was now or never.

Sergeant Leary flicked a look toward the women and children. Mrs. Burns was with them this time, sitting on the ground with Esther, leaning against her shoulder.

Esther caught Leary's look and nodded, once. She put an arm around Mrs. Burns.

At that moment the *Skylark* appeared, just clearing the treetops at the back edge of the clearing, the jungle muffling the sound of its engine until it suddenly flew into sight.

It dropped lower as it winged across the clearing, its abrupt appearance freezing every enemy trooper in the base with shock. Which was its chief function in this operation.

Qualey aimed the plane for the personnel shelters. It was impossible for Nora to achieve much accuracy with the grenades she was holding ready in her hands. It was up to him to keep well away from their own people.

The *Skylark* roared past the watchtower, almost level with the two stunned men on top of it. Qualey had the plane flying as slow as it could, but it was still going too fast for Nora to lob a grenade at the two men and their machine gun. By the time the men unfroze and grabbed for the machine gun, the *Skylark* was already past the tower, flying low over the personnel shelters.

Nora pulled the pins of two grenades and dropped them out the cabin window.

The first hit the roof of a shelter and did little more than frighten the enemy troopers in it as the roof blew apart. But the second hit the ground beside another shelter and bounced into it, killing every man inside with its booming explosion.

Nora instantly snatched up two more grenades, pulled the pins—and threw them out as Qualey flew over the hulk. One hit the deck and killed two enemy troopers with the concussion and flying shrapnel of its blast. The other exploded in the river, throwing up a great geyser of water.

The *Skylark* winged out over the river, leaving behind it the havoc and confusion the prisoners needed.

The four guards had broken out of their surprise and twisted away from the prisoners to look toward the river, raising their rifles in readiness to fire upward as they watched the plane circle to come back.

Sergeant Leary and Soames drew the pistols from inside their shirts, followed a split second later by the oil driller and the British trooper. Point-blank, they fired into the backs of the four guards, blasting them to the ground. They kept pumping shots into them until none were moving.

Tengal, the Eurasian planter, the Dutchman, and his son were already scrambling on their knees, snatching up the four fallen rifles. The Dutchman stayed on one knee, quickly sighting on the two enemy troopers stationed at the machine gun near the edge of the clearing. They were turning the machine gun on the prisoners when he fired his first shot.

It smashed a hole through the forehead of one of them. The other twisted to get away. The Dutchman's second shot caught him in the hip and dropped him. The third went into his chest and killed him.

His son, the planter, and Tengal were firing their rifles at the two men with the machine gun on top of the tower. Their fire was not as accurate as the Dutchman's, but one slug from the first ragged barrage knocked one of the machine gunners off the tower. The other dropped flat on the platform where their bullets could not get at him, but where he couldn't get at the machine gun.

Soames sprinted to the tower and began climbing it, the Enfield .38 revolver clutched in his fist.

That left the machine gun beside the dock, and the one on the last MTB in line.

FIFTEEN

Shaw and Flood came out from under the end of the dock, straightening with their bare feet sunk ankle-deep in mud.

The two men stationed in the stern of the MTB nearest them were firing one of its machine guns at the *Skylark*, which was doing a return swing above the jungle on the other side of the river. The men at the machine gun beside the maintenance shed were doing the same. Both machine-gun teams had their backs to Shaw and Flood.

The two of them climbed onto the dock, not worrying about being noisy at it. The blasting roar of the machine guns covered any sound they made. Flood tucked the spare magazine under his left armpit and pulled the pin of his grenade as Shaw took aim with the Thompson submachine gun.

Shaw squeezed the trigger and swung the tommy gun in a short, low arc as it jumped and stuttered in his hands. A burst of eight steel-jacketed slugs stitched across the backs of the machine gunners on the torpedo boat, flinging their dying bodies away into the river.

Flood threw the grenade carefully. It landed right behind the other machine gunners. They didn't even hear it hit the dirt through the clatter of their machine gun. The explosion and the shrapnel shredding them apart put them beyond hearing.

Shaw tossed the tommy gun to Flood and climbed aboard the torpedo boat, heading for the machine guns. Flood sprinted ten yards along the dock to where he could look down the length of the clearing. He came to a twisting stop as he saw men coming out of the maintenance shed, rushing to the unmanned machine gun next to it. Flood squeezed the trigger as he swung the tommy gun at them.

The slashing bullets flung two of them to the ground and sent the rest scrambling away behind the protection of the shed.

The camp's commander appeared in the doorway of the bungalow, a pistol in his hand. Flood spun and fired at him. Two bullets spat out of the submachine gun, and then the magazine was empty. The commander vanished inside. Flood couldn't tell if he jumped back or was knocked back. He was busy disengaging the empty magazine.

Dropping it on the dock, he quickly attached the spare magazine. As he did so, a bullet slashed the back of his right thigh. He fell to his knees with a grimace of agony, almost dropping the tommy gun. More bullets chopped chunks of wood from the dock in front of him. He turned his head and looked for the source.

Rifles were being fired at him from the deck of the tanker. But Shaw was already at one of the machine guns on the MTB, swinging it around toward the tanker. Aiming upward, he let go a thundering barrage that drove the marksmen away from the tanker's railing.

Flood lurched to his feet and looked back into the clearing. The prisoners were already on the move towards the shelter of the newly built quarters for the MTB crews.

Flood ran limping to the end torpedo boat, blood running down his leg.

Enemy troopers were pouring out of the personnel shelters now, armed and no longer frozen with surprise. The prisoners were hurrying in the opposite direction, toward the shelters they'd finished that day. The women and children led the way; Mrs. Ruyter holding her children by the hands as they ran, Esther helping Mrs. Burns to stay on her feet as they followed. The men brought up the rear, their bodies shielding the women and children, pausing to fire back at the enemy troopers.

But the enemy was firing now too. And with increasing accuracy. Two bullets cut the planter down. Another broke the Dutchman's arm.

Sergeant Leary stopped and threw his grenade, as hard as he could. It fell among the enemy troopers, killing three and momentarily scattering the others. The Dutch trooper threw his, adding to the havoc. The American private was about to toss his when Leary stopped him: "Hold on to it!"

They ran after the other prisoners. Behind them, the enemy troopers started to recover, only to be scattered again as Shaw turned the torpedo boat's machine gun on them.

But Shaw had to quickly switch back to the snipers on the deck of the tanker.

On the watchtower, Soames had reached the top rung. Bending at the knees and hanging on with his left hand, he abruptly straightened with the .38 revolver ready in his right fist. The enemy machine gunner stretched flat on the top platform was looking directly into his eyes when Soames shot him in the top of the head. Soames went up onto the platform as the enemy's face smacked down on the floor. Grabbing at the machine gun, he swung it downward, triggering off a hail of lead at the enemy troopers below, smashing them back, dropping them, sending the survivors scrambling to cover between the personnel shelters.

And in that moment the *Skylark* came winging over the shelters again. This time Nora dropped a string of five grenades out the cabin window as they flew over. She looked down and saw them falling away from her like black eggs of death, the primers clicking as they fell. She saw the enemy troopers among the shelters racing in all directions to get away as the live grenades tumbled to the ground among them, bouncing high.

The multiple booming explosions bowled men over like tiny dolls, hurled several into the air with chunks of the shelters. One of the shelters collapsed completely. The dazed survivors picked themselves up off the ground and began firing after the *Skylark*. The next second the plane vanished, flying low over the jungle at the rear edge of the clearing.

The prisoners had reached the protection of the new MTB crew quarters, shielded by them from the erratic fire of the enemy survivors around the bombed personnel shelters. But ahead of them lay a long stretch of open ground, between them and the bungalow and dock. And now enemy reinforcements were pouring from the hulk and tanker, rushing into the clearing to cut them off.

On the end torpedo boat, Shaw turned the machine gun on these reinforcements. A short burst used up the last of its ammo. He jumped to the other machine gun mounted on the stern, and got it into action. The steady stream of rapid-fire from it, slashing back and forth, mowed down the nearest reinforcements and drove the others for cover. Below him, he could hear Flood working swiftly inside the MTB to get the great engines started, ignoring his bleeding, agony-torn leg.

Atop the watchtower, Soames had also swung his machine gun on the enemy reinforcements. He sent two long bursts into them before the gun abruptly ran out of ammunition. There was no spare ammo for it on the tower. The base camp had never been set up to beat off an attack of any proportions; such a possibility not occurring to anyone at this stage of the war. Soames left the machine gun, and began scrambling down the ladder.

A bullet smashed his groin. His legs slipped from the rungs and hung dangling. He held on with both hands to a rung above, the pain scalding upwards through his body. He was a stationary target now, and the bullets tore into him with vindictive fury.

He was already dead when he fell. He struck the ground flat on his back, his empty eyes staring up at the darkening sky.

The rest of the prisoners were making a run across the open stretch from the MTB crew quarters toward the dock, aiming to circle around the side of the commander's bungalow to the end torpedo boat. The men moved in a wedge, with the three women and two children protected inside it and Sergeant Leary leading the way. But the reinforcements from the tanker and hulk had reformed and were being joined by the survivors from among the personnel shelters. They angled into the clearing after the prisoners, swinging wide to get away from Shaw's machine gun fire.

The *Skylark* reappeared, flashing low over the clearing at them. The enemy formation broke apart as it bore down on them. But the next instant it was flying over their heads, six bunched grenades spilling from it.

The booming flashes of the grenade explosions shattered the charge across the clearing to pieces.

The prisoners, slowed by Esther half carrying Mrs. Burns, approached the commander's bungalow. The American private sprinted up beside Sergeant Leary, hefting the remaining grenade. Suddenly shots were fired at them from the bungalow's rear window.

The private stumbled and gasped as bullets tore his stomach open. Sergeant Leary snatched the grenade from his hand as he went down. The next shot gouged Leary's hip, spinning him to the ground. He hit, rolled, and came up on one knee—pulling the grenade's pin with his teeth.

He had played a lot of baseball in his time, but he never made a better throw in his life. The grenade went in through one of the bungalow's rear windows. There were cries of alarm from inside. Cries that were snuffed out in the roaring flash of the grenade exploding in a confined area, the force of it kicking out half of the bungalow's rear wall.

Sergeant Leary staggered to his feet and led the way around the far side of the now silent bungalow.

On the end torpedo boat, Flood had the engines going. Rushing out onto the deck, he cast off the mooring lines— and saw that the prisoners were pinned down behind the side corner of the bungalow by fire from three enemy troopers beside the maintenance shed. He suddenly realized that the MTB's machine gun was no longer firing. Twisting around, he saw Shaw running from the stern.

"It's jammed!" Shaw snarled at him.

Flood ducked inside the cabin and popped back out, throwing the submachine gun to Shaw. As Flood started back into the cabin, a bullet struck his already wounded leg. This one broke it.

Sprawling face down inside the cabin, Flood began dragging himself across the cockpit. He reached the helmsman's chair, got hold of the seat with both hands, and hauled himself up, balancing on one leg. He sank onto the high seat of the swivel chair, his face contorted and pale. With fumbling hands, he began yanking at one of his shirt sleeves, ripping it off to make a tourniquet.

Outside on the deck, Shaw sprinted to the stern of the MTB. From there he could see the three enemy troopers pinning down the prisoners with their rifle fire. Holding the submachine gun low, he sliced a long deadly burst at them, expending the last of the magazine's cartridges. The slashing bullets broke one of the enemy troopers in half and kicked the legs out from under another. The third made a dash for cover, losing his rifle as he fled.

Shaw sprinted back to the cabin, and inside, strode to the cockpit to help tighten the improvised tourniquet high on Flood's smashed leg. Flood let him do it, grasping the wheel tightly with both hands to control the raging pain.

"Thanks. . . ." He got the word out through clenched teeth.

"Thanks, hell!" Shaw rasped. "You've still got a job to do!"

Sergeant Leary started to lead the prisoners out across the dock. He jumped back fast as bullets chopped into the dock between him and the end MTB.

Rifle shots from the tanker.

But the *Skylark* was already banking towards the tanker, winging low over the length of it, live grenades spilling from it and bounding across the decks. None of them exploded close enough to kill anyone. But the combined effect of their lethal blasts sent all the snipers scurrying for cover for a few precious moments. Long enough for the prisoners to make their final break.

The *Skylark* executed a tight turn for another run at the tanker. It was one too many. Bullets fired from the tanker's deckhouse clanged into the radial engine as the plane nosed down at it.

Qualey heard and felt them, and groaned even before the engine abruptly changed from a roar to an erratic stutter. Rigid with sudden terror, he twisted the controls, heading off at an angle down river, trying to gain altitude.

The engine gave a last stutter and conked out entirely. The prop froze in position. The plane plunged toward the water. Nora hung on to her wicker chair with both hands and shut her eyes tightly as the water rushed up at them. Qualey, pitting all his strength against the stick, managed to get the plane into a semblance of a glide, inches above the river where it flowed through the mangrove swamp to the sea. In the last second, he got the nose up.

The *Skylark* splashed down in an almost perfect landing, but too hard. The hastily repaired pontoon collapsed. The plane tilted over on its left side and began to sink.

As the cabin filled with water, Nora managed to kick the door open. She dove out into the river.

Qualey floundered out after her, yelling something that was drowned as water filled his mouth. He spat it out and tried again. Nora just barely made it out: "I can't swim!"

Twisting around in the river, she saw his arms thrashing

the surface frantically, his face going under. Reaching back with one hand, she grabbed a fistful of the front of his shirt. Dragging him after her, his face still under water most of the time, she swam back to the plane's fuselage. She caught hold of it with her other hand, praying it would stay afloat.

The prisoners were scrambling aboard the torpedo boat, shoving into the cabin and cockpit. Tengal got to the cockpit first, moving straight toward the controls. He stopped when he saw that Flood was already there, sitting on the steering stool with Shaw standing taut-faced beside him. Then he saw Flood's condition and moved closer, offering to take over.

Flood shook his head. He didn't want to try getting any more words than were absolutely necessary past his pain-clenched teeth. He nodded at the throttle controls.

Tengal took up a position there, his hands ready on them.

The men were already getting the women and children down the ladder to the safety of the charthouse and crew quarters below. Esther pulled back when she saw Flood's face. Her eyes quickly dropped to his ruined leg.

She hurried over and fell to her knees beside him. She began ripping his blood soaked trouser leg open.

"No!" Flood shrieked through his teeth. "Not yet! Wait!"

Esther sat down on the deck beside the steering stool, staring at the blood running down and dripping from his bare foot.

Bullets from the tanker began chopping into the forward deck of the MTB they'd commandeered. Enemy troopers appeared again, running in zigzag crouches towards the dock.

"Full astern port!" Flood rasped.

Tengal's hands tightened quickly on the throttle controls.

The twin exhausts belched smoke from the stern as the reversed port engine roared to life. The torpedo boat raced away from the dock, curving backward into the middle of the river.

Flood twisted the wheel. "Both!"

Tengal brought the starboard engine to life, easing up on the port engine.

The MTB straightened out, roaring backwards down the river.

Shaw looked back beyond the stern, and saw the small figures of Nora and Qualey sitting on top of the plane's wing near the mouth of the river. That was all of the plane that was above water: the wing, and the nose with the faded name painted on it: SKYLARK.

Beside Shaw, Sergeant Leary was staring in the opposite direction, at the fast-diminishing base camp.

"We did it," he whispered unbelievingly. "We really did it. . . ." He leaned against the bulkhead, holding his torn hip.

"Not quite," Shaw said meaningfully, and looked pointedly at Flood. "Not yet."

"When I say," Flood told Shaw through his teeth, "push those. . . ." Taking a hand from the wheel, he pointed to two buttons on the cockpit control panel.

Shaw quickly shifted into position near them.

Flood got the hand on the wheel again. "Full ahead both!"

Tengal spread his feet wide apart, and shoved the controls into forward position.

The whole vessel bucked and lurched, coming to a momentary stop in the middle of the river as the huge engines whined with the strain of shifting abruptly from full speed astern to full speed ahead. The next second the MTB lurched forward.

Flood turned the wheel slightly as the torpedo boat raced back up the river, the bows lifting high out of the water and throwing a foaming wake to either side. The point of the bow swung slightly in response to his touch at the wheel. The MTB was now aimed straight at the tanker, closing in on it at maximum speed, the engines thundering.

There were men manning the machine guns on the three MTBs left at the dock now. A slashing hail of bullets thudded into the raised bows, caved in the windows at the top of the cockpit.

The men standing in the cockpit ducked low. Flood stayed exactly where he was, hunching forward a little, both hands gripping the wheel till his knuckles turned white. He watched the nearing tanker dead ahead with eyes like metallic slits.

"Half speed. . . ."

Tengal responded instantly, throttling down.

The MTB slowed, its bow lowering in the water.

Flood shot a look at Shaw. "Now!"

Shaw punched the two buttons with his thumbs, firing the torpedoes.

The torpedoes shot out of the tubes on either side, hit the surface of the river, and streaked ahead of the MTB, straight toward the tanker next to the dock.

As soon as they were well on their way, Flood spun the wheel. The torpedo boat swung away in a tight-turning circle—with all the machine guns on the other three MTBs firing at it at close range.

Bullets whined through the cockpit. Three of them slammed into Flood's chest and kicked him out of the steering stool.

Tengal was into it grabbing the wheel as Flood flopped on the deck. Esther crawled to Flood with a stifled cry, her hands joining his in pawing at the blood gushing from the terrible wounds.

The torpedo boat raced away, back down the river toward the now almost totally submerged *Skylark*. Shaw twisted to look the other way, beyond the stern—in time to see the torpedoes punch into the hull of the tanker.

The explosion was incredible. The whole tanker rose in the water and broke wide apart into separate sections, scattering its flaming fuel all over the dock, the hulk, the three remaining MTBs, and the rest of the base.

Shaw and the others stared in awe as the ammunition on the supply hulk blew up next, adding to the devastation. The force of the two major explosions came across the water, pushing air ahead of them, hitting the people in the fleeing torpedo boat like soft fists. The flames and smoke of the annihilated base gushed skyward, shot through below with sudden flashes as the MTBs at the dock blew up, one after the other.

Tengal slowed the boat to a stop against the slow-sinking wing of the *Skylark*. Nora and Qualey quickly climbed from the wing onto the deck of the boat. Shaw took Nora in his arms and held her to him tightly, not giving a damn what anyone thought. She rested her head against his chest wearily for a long moment, and clung to him as he turned with her back into the cockpit.

Qualey followed them in, sticking close to Shaw.

"That's very nice for you," he told Shaw, "but I just lost my plane on account of you. You better not forget that promise you made me."

"I won't forget it," Shaw said flatly.

And then Qualey and Nora saw Flood lying on the deck inside, with Esther sitting beside him, holding a wadded cloth to his chest. The cloth and her hands were dyed red with his blood.

Flood rolled his head on the deck and stared up bleakly at Shaw. "You can forget your promise to *me*," he whispered. "You don't have to shoot me, after all."

Shaw looked from Flood to Esther, his face hard and questioning.

"If we can get him to a hospital quickly . . ." she started. Her voice trembled and she couldn't finish it. Nor could she fight back the tears.

Flood rolled his head and looked at her with dazed eyes. "Hey . . ." he whispered ". . . you know . . . you're a very pretty girl. . . ."

SIXTEEN

The Vitiaz Straits were open that night. The captured torpedo boat, with its rescued prisoners, swung south below the straits, joining the first of the escape vessels from the north sailing through that opening. They extended back as far as the eye could see in the starlit darkness, a long line of ships coming through to safety and freedom.

But the one who had made it possible could no longer see what he had accomplished.

The man who called himself Sam Flood was dead.